Isabel's hands

Jackie went on, "Anna can have us both. Love us both." She paused to get her voice under control. "And she'll be a better person. Because of me." She smiled. "And because of you."

Isabel felt her eyes grow hot. She felt how cold her fingers were and how goosebumps rose along her spine and down her arms at Jackie's words.

The children's mother lifted her glass in a toast. "I have their past," she told Isabel. "You can have their future."

. . . Isabel's bottle began to shake . . .

JULIA ROBERTS   SUSAN SARANDON
ED HARRIS

CHRIS COLUMBUS

STEPMOM

COLUMBIA PICTURES ᴾᴿᴱˢᴱᴺᵀˢ WENDY FINERMAN ᴾᴿᴼᴰᵁᶜᵀᴵᴼᴺ ᴬ 1492 ᴾᴵᶜᵀᵁᴿᴱˢ "STEPMOM" JENA MALONE ᴹᵁˢᴵᶜ ᴮʸ JOHN WILLIAMS
ᴱˣᴱᶜᵁᵀᴵᵛᴱ ᴾᴿᴼᴰᵁᶜᴱᴿˢ PATRICK McCORMICK · RON BASS · MARGARET FRENCH ISAAC · JULIA ROBERTS · SUSAN SARANDON · PLINY PORTER
ˢᵀᴼᴿʸ ᴮʸ GIGI LEVANGIE · ˢᶜᴿᴱᴱᴺᴾᴸᴬʸ ᴮʸ GIGI LEVANGIE ᴬᴺᴰ JESSIE NELSON · STEVEN ROGERS · KAREN LEIGH HOPKINS ᴬᴺᴰ RON BASS
ᴾᴿᴼᴰᵁᶜᴱᴰ ᴮʸ WENDY FINERMAN · MARK RADCLIFFE · MICHAEL BARNATHAN ᴰᴵᴿᴱᶜᵀᴱᴰ ᴮʸ CHRIS COLUMBUS ᴄᴼᴸᵁᴹᴮᴵᴬ PICTURES

STEPMOM

A novel by Maggie Robb

Based on a Story by Gigi Levangie
Screenplay by Gigi Levangie and
Jessie Nelson & Steven Rogers &
Karen Leigh Hopkins and Ron Bass

WARNER BOOKS

A Time Warner Company

If you purchase this book without a cover you should be aware that this book may have been stolen property and reported as "unsold and destroyed" to the publisher. In such case neither the author nor the publisher has received any payment for this "stripped book."

WARNER BOOKS EDITION

Copyright © 1998 by Columbia Pictures Industries, Inc.
All rights reserved.

Motion picture artwork and photos ©1998 Columbia Pictures Industries, Inc.
All rights reserved

Warner Books, Inc.
1271 Avenue of the Americas
New York, NY 10020

Visit our Web site at
http://warnerbooks.com

W A Time Warner Company

Printed in the United States of America

First Printing: December, 1998

10 9 8 7 6 5 4 3 2 1

ATTENTION: SCHOOLS AND CORPORATIONS
WARNER books are available at quantity discounts with bulk purchase for educational, business, or sales promotional use. For information, please write to: SPECIAL SALES DEPARTMENT, WARNER BOOKS, 1271 AVENUE OF THE AMERICAS, NEW YORK, N.Y. 10020.

STEPMOM

Years from now, looking back, it would appear to be nothing but a progression of days, nothing but summer turning into autumn and autumn into winter. It would be only the season when the light constricts and the darkness looms, and there are lessons in the darkness.

Anna, when she was grown, would think back on these months and be surprised that the span was only months. Living it, the time had passed like years: the way an hour can seem like a day, a day like a week, a week like a year when you are eleven—or when your life is changing forever. She would remember not only the words and the images but also the texture of these months, and they would be recalled to her when she woke with her fingertips running over the picture quilt, or when she touched a puppy's new fur, or when the first snowflake landed on her forehead.

For Ben, it would be different. The photographs would be his memory, most of it. Of course he would know the facts and the dates, would have been told those. He would know what had happened. But it would be mostly darkness in his mind, and the only lighted scenes would be those from the photographs that Isabel had taken, or from the videotape she had shot.

For a long time, many years, he would believe this to be true—that he didn't remember much on his own. But coming up out of sleep or falling down into it, he would sometimes see something so vividly that he could hear it too. It would be his mother singing "Ain't No Mountain High Enough" into a curling iron, or the police officer's face peering at him, or Isabel at his bedside in the hospital singing a song about never leaving him. And later, the next visit with his sister, he would ask her for a copy of that photograph or tape, and Anna would say there was no photograph of that particular event. There was nothing saved at all.

So Ben would come in time to understand that there were some moments he did remember from that season of darkness. He would begin to understand that there were some moments, even then, that shed their own light.

ISABEL

It wasn't that she didn't hear the alarm. It was only that it was one of those late-summer mornings—the lemony light beyond her closed eyes and the one cool breeze of the day brushing along the length of her bare arms and the sheer weight of the summer linens—that made Isabel want to roll over into Luke's arms for just a few more minutes, made her want to stretch alongside him and watch him open his eyes to see her all over again, like new, and smile. It wasn't that she didn't hear the alarm, but only that she didn't yet hear the voice it would summon, the shrill little harpy in her head that soon enough would remind her that Luke was already up and out, and that today was her huge Valentino shoot (meaning Duncan was hyped beyond all reason), and that she had to get the kids . . .

Her eyes opened, swung to the time. It was 7:45. She sat up, threw her legs over the side of the bed, and ran for the door in one blur of light-headed motion—only interrupting her momentum long enough to grab her flannel robe off the chair. She slept wearing nothing but a pair of Luke's boxers and a loose tee shirt. And all she needed was to traumatize the kids with a peek of bare flesh. Wouldn't that go over in a major way?

She hesitated, deciding which one of them to wake first, and it cost her vital seconds. She had to remind herself that they were only kids: rugrats, munchkins, pipsqueaks, punks.

Pounding up the stairs, which really fuel-injected the adrenaline, she headed for Ben's room. At seven, he was the younger of the two. And although it sometimes seemed a miscalculation, she imagined that his being younger made him the more forgiving. "Ben," she said to the lump in the bed. "You overslept again!"

Stepping around the stuff on his floor—it was as though one of his magic tricks had exploded in here—she began to rifle through his clothing to find something, anything that was presentable enough for school. This was why Luke had told her you were supposed to do it the night before. "Get everything laid out at bedtime," he'd said one night, as he made a show of draping the shirt over the back of the chair and laying the pants out in the seat and stuffing a sock into each of the two shoes. So that it looked like an empty version of Ben, just waiting for somebody to blow life into him. If she had listened, Isabel wouldn't have found herself where she was now: late and unable to lay her hands on anything clean that matched anything else. "Get up, get up, get up!" she chanted frantically.

Ben wasn't moving. And he had to be doing it to spite her. Nobody could sleep through the decibels of her alarm. So much for his being the more forgiving of the two. "Ben, you're late. I'm serious. I'm wearing a very serious face."

He didn't make a move to see for himself whether she was or wasn't.

"Don't make me start counting."

Nothing.

"ONE." She tugged the sleeve of a shirt hanging on a chair, and a bouquet of flowers bounced out. She flipped it over her shoulder. "TWO." And, gross, what had he left in the shirt pocket, a dirty handkerchief? God, she couldn't send him off like this. She'd never hear the end of it. Never, never. She yanked the handkerchief, and it came out and out and out, another of his tricks—blue then red then orange then purple. "Don't make me say three," she said to the bed. "I'm about to say three. THREE!"

He didn't stir. And she wondered—couldn't help but wonder—how Luke could do this to her, though she instantly berated herself for blaming Luke, then blamed herself for being undone by a little boy/rugrat. She just had to be firm with him, that's all. She had to let him feel how truly in charge she was of the situation, and of him. Bending down, she ripped off his covers like a magic trick of her own. Only it turned out to be another of Ben's tricks. There was his blowup dinosaur. But no Ben.

"Ben," she said to the general mess of the room. "I'm not kidding around. You make yourself appear *this instant*."

Something touched her foot. God, he was hiding under the bed again. He had tried that twice last week alone; she should've thought of it. She prepared her stern face and crouched to retrieve him, then screamed. It was only the damned white bunny that Ben used when he was in his magician mode, the damned sneaky bunny that never got put in its cage and consequently had a talent for pooping precisely wherever it was that Isabel was going to put her bare foot. "You think this is funny, but this is actually not funny," she said, as much to the rabbit as to the boy hiding, wherever he was.

She shuffled around in the closet before giving up and hopping over the bunny, around a zillion toys, and toward the door, where she stubbed her baby toe while trying to miss a leaning tower of books. Limping in agony, she headed down the stairs to the door with the encouraging greeting in all caps, KEEP OUT EVERYONE! Isabel knew this included her most of all, or maybe only her. But she opened the door anyway. Munchkins, pipsqueaks.

Eleven-year-old Anna was sitting on the edge of her bed.

"Good," Isabel told her, smiling. "You're already up."

Anna did not smile back. In fact she looked so furious that Isabel could hardly see any softness left over from sleep. Isabel knew there could be softness about Anna. Sometimes late at night, when the kids were in bed, Isabel looked in on them and saw them in the wedge of light thrown by the open door. She saw their sweetness then, their smooth beauty and vulnerability. She saw what they never gave her a chance to see otherwise—and surely what Luke saw in them always. But it was vanished now. Anna, in full snit, held up her purple tee shirt.

Uggghhh, Isabel realized, quick as a slap. She had forgotten the laundry, too.

Anna said, "You forgot to wash my purple shirt. I told you a hundred times it was Purple Shirt Day at school today."

Isabel tried to recover. "I didn't forget. I was up all night thinking about it . . ."

The girl wasn't buying it. "Right," Anna said, and Isabel couldn't believe how much sarcasm could be crammed into one syllable.

Isabel kept riffing, ". . . and I concluded that you're too special to look like everyone else." She tossed Anna a tee shirt the color of a blood orange. "Orangey red. That's your color. Few can carry it off. Now please help me find your brother."

"You lost Ben?"

"Of course not," Isabel said. "Does he look lost to you?"

She left Anna's room—retreated really—and called the boy's name all the way into the kitchen. There was no sign of him. He hadn't been into the donuts or the boxes of cereal—Froot Loops, Cocoa Puffs, Cheerios—that Luke had lined up on the counter before he left to go face his workload. Even with a big case on his mind, Luke could still remember the kids' cereal. So what was wrong with her?

Popping a can of Diet Coke, the first truly good event of her day, she flung open the pantry door. This was getting to her. Wasn't it hard enough for her without them making it harder, without them making it into an obstacle course that she could never make it through because . . .

Anna came in and flopped herself onto a counter stool. At least she had put on the orangey-red tee shirt. But then what choice did she have? It was probably the only clean scrap of clothing she had with her, the poor kid. Thinking this, which only made Isabel more irritated and as much at herself as at either one of the kids, she said, "Come on, Ben. Goddammit."

"You swore," Anna said.

The toaster popped, and Isabel grabbed at the toast and tried to put stone-cold butter on it, which only shredded and mashed it. The kitchen clock said 7:56. Panicked, Isabel flung the piece of toast in front of Anna, who whined: "No, I told you. I like apple butter. Not butter butter."

Isabel handed her an apple.

"Never mind," Anna said. "I'll just eat my lunch."

Another realization poked Isabel hard between the eyes: "Lunch." She had completely spaced on making their sack lunches. Opening the fridge, she reached for meat and mayo, then hauled the bread off the counter.

Anna said, "You forgot to make my lunch?" There was a question mark on the end of it. But there was no question in the kid's tone. Isabel wondered if there were any judge in the world more damning than an eleven-year-old? God, it was easier dealing with Duncan's towering pain-in-the-ass ego than with Anna.

"No," Isabel defended herself, denying the obvious. "I'm almost done making it."

"Don't lie. I'll get hot lunch."

"I'll make it." And she would, while simultaneously making a speech to the room: "All right, Ben. Fine. You explain to your teacher why you're late. You write yourself a note. Your daddy told you he had an important case this morning, and he had to leave early, and we were . . ." She ripped off a sheet of foil, turned on one foot to get a butter knife, then swung back around, reaching for a cupboard door. Opening it, she screamed in surprise.

There was Ben, holding out the peanut butter.

"Shit!" she yelped.

His laughter exploded, and he almost tumbled out. His little eyes were burning with the thrill of it. If she hadn't been able to see Luke in that silly grin of his—loud and clear—she'd have dragged him out of there and dropped the little squeaker on his head.

"Ben," she said, "that is *so* not funny. You're late. Really late. Now get out here and have some cereal."

"No."

"Fine. Eat in the cupboard." She handed him a bowl of cereal and went back to making Anna's lunch. Still, she could see him up there, poking through his cereal, looking all disappointed.

"No," he insisted autocratically. "Cocoa Puffs on top. Froot Loops on the bottom."

Isabel grabbed the bowl—she'd really had it now—turned it upside down on the countertop, which reversed the order of the cereal. Then, she swept it back into the bowl and quickly handed it back to him even as the phone began to ring.

"You touched it," he accused her.

"Then have a donut."

"There's only jelly. I hate jelly."

"Then starve," she told him, and knew instantly that it sounded way past flip and all the way into harsh. But she couldn't help herself because they were late, she was late, and the damned phone was ringing.

"I'm gonna beep Daddy at work," Anna retaliated.

"He's badgering a witness," Isabel told her. "Eat."

"But you told us to starve."

Isabel answered the phone. It was her boss, Duncan. He was tense times thirty. "The ad agency's already there?" she echoed him, buying herself time, trying to find a way to buy some goodwill as well. "I'm out the door."

Ben aimed a Froot Loop at her.

"Knock it off," she told him. Then she told Duncan not to worry. "It's gonna go beautifully," she said, infusing her voice with confidence.

Ben shot off another Froot Loop.

Isabel kept the phone crooked against her shoulder as she threw the lunch production into overdrive: She scrapped the sandwich idea and put into action the leftover plan. She emptied last night's cold pizza and HoHo's and Doritos into the only available bags she had—a plastic Duane Reade from when she bought tampons yesterday and an oversize brown paper one with some kind of grease stain. But, *c'est la vie,* the clock already said 8:00.

As Duncan was reciting his concern over whether the creative team—meaning Isabel—would pull off the crucial sophistication in one of Isabel's ears, Anna said to the other, "Did you remember my egg carton?"

"Hold on," Isabel told Duncan. "Egg carton?" she asked Anna.

"I told you I needed my egg carton for seed planting today." Anna's hands were on her hips.

Isabel kept humming her presence into the phone, yessing and noing Duncan, comforting his neuroses even as she opened the fridge and pulled out a carton of eggs. "Absolutely, Duncan. I'm on top of everything."

She dumped the eggs, and missed the sink. Of course. The eggs shattered on the floor with a squishing *pop pop pop*. "Damn," she said inside her head. She shoved the empty carton at Anna.

"Eggzactly," she said to Duncan. "I'm putting on my coat."

As she hung up, the panic surged into her veins, pure adrenaline. "We are late. We are seriously late. Which means, Mister Ben, we've got to get you dressed."

Ben leapt out of the cupboard and tried to race away, but Isabel was so pumped by now that she lunged for him, nabbed him. He wiggled as she struggled to get his pajama bottoms peeled free of his feet. She had to wrestle him to the floor, and by the time she had his head tragically stuck in his twisted pajama top, his school clothes had dropped into the egg goo.

Isabel thought she might explode then. She even imagined hearing the sound of her own detonation. But it was only the knock at the door, only the solid three-stroke knock that she had been dreading ever since the harpy inside her head overrode Pete Townsend on the radio-alarm and reminded her that getting the kids ready for school was all hers today.

Anna opened the door, and Isabel could do nothing but sprawl on the floor with Ben pinned and squirming half-naked in her arms. She looked up to meet the disapproval in Jackie's eyes.

Jackie Harrison was a woman who could wear yellow—yellow sweater tied around her neck, yellow stripes tucked into sharply creased pants—and yet still look like someone who would be just as comfortable—maybe more so—in gray flannel with patent pumps. Her smile was all sunshine, too, but cloudy underneath, dark and disapproving. Isabel could see it even if no one else could.

"Mommy!" both kids cheered. Anna ran into Jackie's arms as though she was nothing at all but a little angel.

"You look like you're having fun, Ben," Jackie said to her son, with her voice too sparkly somehow.

He grinned triumphantly from Isabel's stranglehold. "Mommy," he reported, "Isabel told us to starve."

Rugrats, munchkins, pipsqueaks, Isabel thought, disentangling herself from him. *Punks.*

"I'll take it from here," Jackie told Isabel coolly, efficiently. She gathered them to her, as if to protect them from this woman in men's underwear who had egg white sliding down her shin.

But even as Isabel picked herself up off the floor and rushed off to try to find something to wear herself—when all she really wanted to do was go back to sleep, back to where there were no compromises on happiness—she reminded herself that Jackie might be immaculately dressed and intimidating in her intelligence. She might be beautiful and competent. But she was Luke's ex-wife, stress on *ex.*

Luke was with Isabel now.

And Isabel would do anything for him. She knew this for certain as Jackie took the kids in hand and ushered them toward the elevator. Isabel knew that she would get up in the morning, any morning, even the morning of the biggest shoot of her career thus far, and she would wrestle Ben into clothes and hear Anna's eyes rolling in her head even when her back was turned. Isabel knew that she would wrap leftover pizza in foil for their lunches and wipe splattered egg off her leg and put herself together for work in ten minutes flat and also that she would do it again every Tuesday and Thursday, every alternating weekend. She would do that and whatever else it took to prove not only that she was capable of dealing with those two little kids, but also that she *wanted* to. She wanted to do it for Luke. She *would* do it for Luke.

JACKIE

In the elevator on the way down to the car, Anna leaned against her mother, and Jackie inhaled the salty sweetness that came out of the part on her daughter's hair, that quirky part that had sprung its own way ever since Anna's first haircut. It was the smell of Jackie's baby, that sugared popcorn smell. And breathing it in was the first clear, clean breath Jackie had drawn since Luke had picked the children up the day before. Finally the air reached all the way down to the place where her serenity was coiled against their return, withdrawn and waiting for proof that they were all right. She squeezed Ben's hand and felt the callus he had worn on the ridge of his palm practicing with his magician's wand every night after school. The smell of Anna's hair part, that rough little hand: familiar, safe. They were back with her.

On the street corner, she tossed the sack lunches Isabel had packed. Who in her right mind would give children HoHo's and cold pizza for lunch? It was another thing she was going to have to bring up with Luke. Another thing. Last week it was the F-word suddenly cropping up in Ben's vocabulary, and the week before that it was Anna's new taste for

Diet Coke. Which wasn't good for growing bones. And, no, she couldn't just ignore it.

As she strapped the children into the Volvo, the street was already shaking off its early-morning languor, starting to percolate at a New York boil. Even down here in Soho, where the beautiful people affected a sort of California ease with themselves and their prospects, even here, it was still boiling-point New York. And Jackie felt the city's old heat lapping at her, warming her up to that hot urge to be faster, smarter, richer, thinner, younger. She could feel it (pervasive as that inexplicable burnt-coffee smell that was so strong here on some days) and with it, she could feel all the reasons she had wanted to leave, to whisk her babies off to the suburbs to grow up with daffodils they could pick if they wanted to—because they had been planted by their mother and not by the Central Park Conservancy.

Jackie had wanted to move out of the city partly because she had not wanted to hear her old aspirations whispering sibilant seductions to her when she was sitting on the subway with the stroller wedged in between one stranger's briefcase and another's cello. She had not wanted to have any of her attention competing with what was best in her, which was the way she loved Anna and Ben. With Anna's birth, her ambition had transformed itself: She had decided that it was not her destiny to find and publish an American Proust but instead to guide these two children among the truly wonderful things about living, such as snowdrops coming up through the last drifts of winter and horses trotting just fast enough for the wind to blow your hair, such as mornings with birdsong.

And not horns. This traffic was a snarl, and horrible. Why had Luke wanted to come back here? Why had he brought the children back, into this, and necessarily drawn Jackie back, too? For years, she had been content in the old gray-and-white Victorian in Nyack, in its yard with the grand old trees and mossy corners. She had been content with picket fences and walks to school and ice cream at the vintage drugstore on Main Street. She had been content to hear the children's voices as they played on the porch while she made their supper just the way they liked it. For years.

Jackie nosed the station wagon out onto the West Side Highway, and for once, the stream of cars was not a halt of brake lights. It flowed, running upstream along the shining Hudson. She felt the relief of the movement. Maybe the kids wouldn't be too late after all, despite the best efforts of that Little Thing their father was living with now. Isabel clearly wasn't capable of caring for them in even the simplest ways. Luke should just give in and hire a nanny to take over when he couldn't be there. He should just admit to himself what was clear to everyone else: Isabel was out of her depth.

That fact was certainly not lost on Anna and Ben. Even now Anna was staring out the window. Distress vibes came off her like heat waves off asphalt in August. Their daughter had always been that way, not so much sulking as thinking it through, turning every angle toward the light.

Jackie handed Anna the lunch bag she had packed for her. Inside were the peanut-butter-and-apricot-jelly on sunflower seed bread, one carrot peeled and cut into three pieces, a dozen red grapes, four graham crackers, and a Hershey's kiss. Just the way Anna liked it. And Ben crowed when Jackie reached into the backseat to give him his lunch. She had found some magician stickers yesterday when she stopped in at the pharmacy. Turning back to the wheel, Jackie spotted trouble just in time and had to dart out of her own lane to avoid a stray shopping cart on the highway.

Ben said, "Why does Isabel wear Daddy's underpants? Doesn't she have underpants of her own?"

Jackie smiled at him in the rearview mirror, but what she said was really meant for Anna. Jackie suspected she knew exactly the reason Anna was so sober this morning. "I noticed a whopping pile of laundry sitting on the washer. Perhaps Isabel's underpants are in there."

"Right next to my purple shirt," Anna said.

Ah-ha, Jackie thought.

Anna's frustration was thick and bitter. "I'm never speaking to her again."

"Never say never." Jackie knew even better than Anna that speaking to her father's new woman was a fact of life. Luke had decreed it, just by loving Isabel (or lusting after her, or whatever). Jackie knew it was her duty to set the tone with the kids. Hostility was no kind of gift. Still, she couldn't always crowd the snideness out of her tone. What was Luke thinking?

"She's always messing up my life," Anna said.

"It's not fair to say always."

"I hate her. She's a witch."

"And no name calling. Use your words."

"I hate when you say that."

"Good. Hate is an acceptable word," she told her daughter, trying to keep an eye on the idiot weaving lanes in a white Lexus. "The word hate should be used with care. Only for things we truly despise."

Ben leaned forward. "Like what?"

Jackie thought for a second, and then said, "Like the planet Uranus. I hate it. Terrible name for a planet." This cracked Ben right up. And got Anna's attention. Jackie went on: "Or the hokey-pokey?"

"The hokey-pokey?" Ben shouted.

"I hate doing the hokey-pokey," Jackie explained. "Especially at weddings. Hate."

Ben said, "I hate cantaloupe."

Jackie said, "I never knew that."

Ben burped, and Anna aimed a glare at him. "I hate when you do that. I can smell what you had for breakfast."

"Excellent point," Jackie agreed, wrinkling her nose. And they all laughed.

Ben said, "I hate sitting in Uncle Stan's lap. He's itchy."

Anna said, "I hate talking to people with food in their teeth when you can't tell them about it."

"I hate pajamas with feet and baking soda in my toothpaste," Ben added.

And, as Jackie pulled up in front of the school, she said, "I hate to say good-bye." She did truly hate it. Especially when she had been with them all of thirty minutes, a good half an hour in which she had dodged a stray shopping cart in the right lane, had swerved to miss a pedestrian, and had been in the wrong lane for her TransPass to register the toll. She had wasted half an hour on the West Side Highway when she might have been walking with them from the house, noticing that the goldenrod was just beginning to turn yellow down by the creek, and that Mrs. Tate had sixteen goldfinches at her thistle feeder, and that Ben's pant legs were showing his socks even though he'd been walking on the hem when summer started. *Oh, Luke,* she thought, *how could you?*

She leaned to kiss each of the children. Ben hugged her around the neck, pecked her on the cheek, then pecked her again on the other. "Be remarkable," she called after him as he crawled out.

Anna sat with her hand on the door release. She was warily watching the other children in her class, who were all wearing purple shirts.

Jackie said, "It's really not so bad, Anna. You're wearing red and blue, and that makes purple. Chromatically you are in the purple family."

Anna gave her a little smile, which said she was not entirely convinced. And then she got out anyway.

Jackie didn't put the car in gear but stayed as Ben ran to the kindergarten playground. He was eager as a puppy to be back with his friends. But Anna was more reluctant, and Jackie watched her ascend the steps to the door, the only orangey red dot in all that purple: her little girl turning into a self-conscious adolescent. It was the toughest age. It had to be.

Only after Anna had disappeared from sight altogether did Jackie put her hands on the wheel and turn the Volvo's wheels from the curb, thinking the hard thought, the thought that had been hardest for her ever since the day she had given birth to Anna.

That morning, the nurses had taken the baby away to clean her up and "book her," as Luke had put it, and Jackie had sobbed from exhaustion and joy, yes, but also from glimpsing the hard truth for the first time: There were going to be some places her children had to go alone, some places she could not follow, some hurts she would not be able to make better with a Flintstones Band-Aid. It was as though some part of her recognized, already knew, that someday her children would have to cope not only with a daddy who left but also with his incompetent young live-in. Or worse.

It was as if some part of Jackie recognized, even then, that Ben would have to learn that no amount of magic would ever undo every lousy thing, and Anna would have to discover—all on her own—that orangey red had a singular beauty, and if she had to, it was a beauty she was equal to carrying off.

ISABEL

If she had to do this without her usual venti mocha frappuccino, so be it. Isabel was late. Bursting through the door of the studio, she tore off her jacket and raced into the midst of the frenzy. She tried not to look harried but to keep her head up and slightly back as if her tardiness just might be calculated to give her the edge here: a muscle play by the capricious photographer.

Even from across the room, she could see that Duncan wasn't buying it. Relief rushed over him at the sight of her. She had clearly had him hanging. But anyway, the show of attitude was more for the restless clients who were gathered around him—the Suits—and she couldn't tell if it played with them. Their aloof expressions were as correct as their tailored clothing.

Probably it didn't play with them either.

Isabel's assistant, Cooper, appeared at her side with one eyebrow up, questioning her through his little rimmed glasses, too cool just to ask outright.

She said, "I had a black bra on with a white shirt and then I couldn't find a black shirt so I had to put on a white bra to go with this shirt."

Cooper never batted an eye. Only semi-grinned. He was serious-minded. One of them had to be.

Isabel took the measure of the scene. Dear Cooper, who was the soul of organization and who had saved her butt more often than she would like to admit, already had the models in place, six gorgeous women wearing red Valentino cocktail dresses. The models were impatient though, she could tell, and hot from the glare of the lights. "Back off the fill," Isabel called to Cooper, even as she got a look through the camera. "I need more shadow."

Okay, she was fine. She was finding her groove. This was a *lot* easier than getting two kids ready for school.

Cooper leaned close. "You've got a Froot Loop in your hair," he said confidentially.

"You say that like I don't know."

He smirked as she fished it out of her hair. "I once threw an entire bowl of potato salad on my stepmother's head."

Isabel switched camera lenses. "And when did that pass?"

"Actually never," Cooper admitted. "I always hated her. Still do. I think there's a gene for it."

She shot him a look, then directed herself to the camera. Through it, she saw a craft service worker balancing a tray of snacks and cool drinks in each hand. The poor guy was balding, short, and overweight, a little round punch line of a man surrounded by models who wanted what he had: cold bottled water and tart apples and coffee cake. His tee shirt was too tight, and he had on black socks with his sneakers. But he was a happy man. The overheated, thirsty models were swarming all over him, reaching for refreshment.

Voilà, Isabel thought, *there it is*. She framed up

the shot, let the automatic advancer roll. This was great.

Duncan pulled himself away from butt-kissing the Suits and walked over to her, trying to signal nonchalance with his body language—for the ad execs—while still getting the point across that he was pissed with her. "Isabel."

She kept working.

"We've been waiting over an hour . . ."

Without taking the camera from her eye, she said, "I'm sorry. It won't happen again."

Impatience was a quaver in his voice, as though his vocal cords were a string instrument with too much tension applied. "Why are you shooting this craft service worker?"

"Because I see something you don't see," she told him. Nothing but the truth.

"We've been waiting for over an hour." He cocked his head discreetly toward the Suits. "The clients have been waiting."

"Duncan. Please. Stand back."

He was getting in her way, and this was the moment. This was . . . He was hanging over her, waiting.

Finally she grinned and told him, "This session's gonna make you remember why you hired me. Even though I wouldn't sleep with you." She pitched her voice a little lower on that, but not so much that it wouldn't make him wonder if anyone else could hear. She didn't take her focus off her work, but he backed off, and if she knew him well— and after all the crap she'd put up with from him, she did—he was smiling that smug smile of his.

There. Done. She rewound the film quickly, popped out the diskette.

"Thanks, guys. That's a wrap," she called out, heading for the exit.

The room went silent. Everyone—the crew, the models, Cooper, Duncan, the Suits—everyone was staring at her in complete bewilderment. Poor Duncan was struggling to keep that signature smile on his face. "This is a joke," he said to her. "Please. Tell me that you're joking." He tried to include everybody in on it, as though it were another of her artistic stunts, another show of attitude. Everyone waited for the punch line.

"Nope. I got it. It's great."

Duncan stared so hard that it almost slipped into a glare, but she held his eye. Total confidence. "Meet me in the conference room in one hour," she told him.

Grabbing Cooper, she rushed off to the darkroom. This was the part she really loved, and when she was finally at the computer console, it was as though she were the kid in third grade again, the kid who colored the stars purple and the moon cobalt and who made everyone else see the night sky the way she saw it—and won first prize in the Grover Cleveland Elementary School art show. That was when she had learned that everything that had made her Isabel—all the good and all the sad—all of that had given her a different way of seeing the same thing that everyone else saw. That was when she started trying to capture her way to show to everyone else.

Now, on the monitor, she pulled up a photo of the craft service worker surrounded by the models.

Then she erased the trays of food from his hands and loaded up another series of photos from the wardrobe shoot they had done the day before. There was Cooper dressed in hip Valentino. She simply removed the jacket and tee shirt from his photo and moved it onto the body of the craft service worker, stretched it to fit, shortened it. It was sort of like playing with Silly Putty and the Sunday funny papers.

"Let's see if I can save both our jobs," she joked, because she could feel Cooper waiting behind her as she did it.

She also felt it when he began to see it the way she saw it. That was what juiced her, his awe, and by the time the two of them sped off to the conference room, she was psyched to see what the response would be.

The room was tense. Duncan had clearly talked himself into silence, and the clients weren't helping him out any. Without a word, Isabel displayed the finished photo: The stubby craft service worker was standing in the middle of the frame wearing not his stretched-to-the-max tee shirt and black socks but sporting instead a Valentino suit and beautiful shoes. With the trays gone from his hands, the worker appeared to be shrugging, a response to his good fortune at being surrounded by six adoring gorgeous models who seemed to be trying to get their hands on him. Isabel had loaded in some copy, which read: VALENTINO. CLOTHES THAT MAKE THE MAN.

Duncan, who never ever had the courage of his own convictions (unless it had to do with trying to score), swiveled to face the clients. The clients meanwhile were looking at the photograph closely, silently. Duncan swung his eyes back to Isabel. She could see he was in a state of throttled-down terror.

But Isabel only smiled and waited for the truth to soak in once more, waited for him to recognize again what she had known since the day she was six and turned the stars purple, what she had known way before she ever fell in love with Luke or met his ex-wife or their two tough little munchkins. She waited for Duncan to recognize what the Suits were even now confirming with smiles and nods: The way she saw the world was worth something.

LUKE

As he geared the car into motion, he thought that nothing surprised him anymore. Nothing. He had his own set of Murphy's Laws worked out, and one of them was that on his most crucial days in court, something would happen with the kids: He would be torn between his responsibilities. It was invariable, especially since the divorce, when he either had to get himself out of the office on Tuesday and Thursday evenings in time to be with the kids, or he had to hire somebody to be there when Jackie brought them, or he had to send a car service after them when Jackie couldn't make the drive. It was all so complicated, but he had argued hard with Jackie for his place in Anna's and Ben's lives, and he didn't mean to let logistics undo his efforts. Of course, Isabel had eased the situation, had insisted with the sweet generosity that shaped her. But even Isabel couldn't take up all the slack. No matter how hard she tried.

Today he had been at work since six-thirty because the judge was threatening a mistrial, and of course at noon Anna's counselor had called. And it couldn't wait. Jackie had already been called, the counselor explained, and the meeting was set for two-thirty. He could be there or not.

And how could he not?

Jackie was the reason it couldn't wait, Luke had thought, as he headed uptown along the West Side Highway—which Giuliani should consider renaming the West Side parking lot. Of course, Jackie was the reason the meeting couldn't wait. If there was a problem, no matter how damned minor, it had to be dealt with two hours ago. Pronto. Couldn't she have at least called him herself and worked out a time when it would have been convenient for both of them? Because now he had no choice but to go at her convenience—whatever feats of wangling it had taken with his partners. Jackie's mood lately was just too dire to screw around with: This thing with Isabel was under her skin.

The cell phone rang. He took the call, but talking to his office got him so fired up that he didn't get into the exit lane early enough, and it cost him vital maneuvering time. When he walked into the school at last, Jackie was already seated in the waiting area, and the counselor was standing in her doorway, checking her watch.

The counselor's name was Ruth Franklin, and she had a scarf knotted around her neck (always a bad sign). She was dark-eyed and serious, very matter-of-fact. As she seated Jackie and Luke in front of her desk, Luke got a flashing sense that the two of them were nothing but overgrown children before this woman's authority. They might have answers of their own; but Ruth Franklin's would always be right. He faced judges every day who didn't unnerve him as much as this brisk little woman in her navy blue pumps. What in the world could have made her call about their Anna, who was a straight-A student and a good little artist, and who was so conscientious about her schoolwork that she read every library book she could for extra credit?

"Mr. and Mrs. Harrison," the counselor began (as though it were an opening statement), "while change is exhilarating for adults, it can be quite challenging for a child."

Luke's beeper went off, and his mind immediately rifled through all the possible scenarios unfolding down in the city—a ruling was in, or there was trouble with a witness or . . . But he didn't allow himself to look at the screen to verify who was calling. He had to ignore it for now. He said, "I won't get that. It's fine." He grinned at Jackie to assure her he was serious, then looked back to Mrs. Franklin. "Change . . . We were talking about change," he prompted her.

Mrs. Franklin nodded and said, "The fact that you two are remarrying obviously has Anna overjoyed . . ."

Luke's eyes locked onto Jackie's; she appeared to be equally dumbfounded. They both looked to Mrs. Franklin for an explanation, both of them grinning uncomfortably, while she blithely carried on, unaware of their shock, ". . . and she's very excited about your move to Switzerland."

Jackie waved a hand and halted her. "She said we're getting remarried?"

Mrs. Franklin nodded and said, "My concern is that Anna seems apathetic toward her work, knowing she's leaving before the semester ends."

"Mrs. Franklin, we're not . . ." Jackie began and before she could finish . . .

Luke added, ". . . planning on getting . . ."

"Remarried." Jackie finished for them both, bluntly, finally. "There is no move."

"Really?" the counselor tried to appear unfazed. "Well, then my concern for . . ."

His beeper went off again. Jackie shot a glance at him, though she tried to cover it with a little smile—that fake little smile that didn't work on him anymore and probably never had. The smile screamed: *Aren't you man enough even to control that rude machine?* But all she said was, "Are you here?" There was the usual accusation in her tone.

"I'm here," Luke told her firmly.

"Because you don't really seem to be here." She was still smiling away, as if he couldn't see right through it.

"I'm here," he said, trying to grin it off. But she was pushing too hard. He had busted his ass to get here for this. "I've got a case where they're this close to sequestering the jury, but have I answered the beeper?" he said.

He was uncomfortably aware of the counselor listening to this exchange. He tried to signal with his eyes that Jackie should tone herself down.

Her response was typical. "So turn it off," she told him.

Luke grin-glared. But he switched off the beeper just to shake her loose. Jackie could be as tenacious as this old dog he'd once had who would hang off a dangled sock for an hour, just to outlast you. Jackie was that brand of stubborn.

They both looked to the counselor, who gathered herself and said, "I'm wondering if there's anything going on at home that could be intensifying Anna's need to create this fantasy?"

Oh, Christ, Luke thought. Jackie would run with this one. He looked at his hands, ignored her glance, and preempted anything his ex-wife would have to say on the issue: "I've been with another woman a little over a year," he explained calmly, "and didn't feel it was appropriate for her to move into my home too quickly. But after a lot of thought and careful discussion with her—and the kids I might add—she moved in last month."

Jackie all but snorted. She told Mrs. Franklin: "In the three short years since our divorce, Luke has seen a number of different women. And without a lot of warning for the children, he's now living with a woman half his age . . ."

"Isabel's not half my age."

"We're not discussing your age."

"Then why bring it up?" He tried to keep it sounding light. He tried to keep up the mild, cheerful facade for the counselor.

"We're discussing the children," Jackie said. "And they want to be with you. They go to your house to be with their father."

"They come to my house to be part of my life. Isabel is part of my life." He was being firm now. He had no choice. She had shoved too hard, as always. He had always tried to be a good father. He knew he tried. She knew it, too, for chrissakes. He loved his children, and they loved him. Dammit, he was an overworked trial lawyer in New York City with an ugly case on his hands that involved powerful people—and yet here he was in this counselor's office in Nyack. For Anna. Couldn't Jackie see what was right before her eyes?

And did she really think this was appropriate,

provoking him to this old back-and-forth? Hanging out the argument that had been going on in their lives for years now—in front of this smug third party? How was this helping their daughter? What about any of this was good for Anna?

The counselor stepped back in. "Mr. Harrison, I hear you talking about your life, your needs. But are you really in touch with what Anna needs?"

He couldn't believe it. Did his presence here mean nothing to anyone? Did everyone think he had just driven up here for kicks in the middle of a god-awful day?

But he didn't blink. He hadn't spent decades in the courtroom without learning control over a situation. "She needs a home where she feels safe and loved. What I'm trying to give her," he told Mrs. Franklin calmly.

"Isn't that what she had?" Jackie sounded bitter, saying that. Jackie sounded as though it was more about herself than about their two children.

His voice thickened, something that never happened to him in the courtroom because he never cared this much. He reminded Jackie of what she damn well knew. He said, "I would walk through fire for Anna and Ben. Gladly. Any day of the week." For emphasis, and Mrs. Franklin's benefit, he struck the desktop with the flat of his hand, hard.

Jackie's eyes swiped at him, flashing indignation. "Except for last Thursday when Isabel forgot to pick them up," she said, flogging away with her list of mistakes.

"Jackie." He couldn't keep the irritation from his tone. "Isabel was five minutes late." He smiled at Mrs. Franklin. He tried to get this back on track.

The counselor inserted herself between them again by saying (and he could have kissed her for this, scarf or no scarf), "I'm wondering if Anna is responding to the underlying hostility that exists between Isabel and Mrs. Harrison."

This struck Jackie mute, Luke noticed. She was suddenly silent. And Luke didn't miss the beat. He said calmly: "Of course she's responding to it. You think it's easy for any of us? You think it's easy for Jackie to watch her kids being looked after by someone who really has no experience being a mother? Of course Jackie's going to be hostile, irrational, and defensive."

He never stopped looking Mrs. Franklin in the eye, but peripherally he saw Jackie's jaw unhinge. "Thank you, Luke," she told him, though she didn't quite muster enough spite. And so he just ended up feeling guilty for having said it. If she'd just lay off him. If she just wouldn't shove so damned much . . .

JACKIE

No denying, this was hard for her, Jackie thought, as she walked along the sidewalk past all the calm houses with their white or rock fences, past their grand old shade trees and their ancient lilacs with heart-shaped leaves: everything so familiar. It was a walk that usually soothed her, the short hike from home to the children's school. Which was the whole reason she had driven home after the meeting with the counselor, parked in the driveway, and started walking back to school to be there when the last bell rang. The thought of hanging around in the corridors, stewing over what had just happened, had depressed her. This walk always did her good.

Damn him.

Since the divorce, Jackie had consistently tried to rebuff the part of herself that still relied on Luke. But it was like some jack-in-the-box in her psyche. And today when the counselor had called, out of the blue like that, she had wanted one thing: to get Luke there and get it taken care of—whatever it was. No matter how ably Jackie handled the day-in-and-day-out of the children's lives, there was still something about an emergency, or even a school counselor's call, that made her want Luke. And fast.

It wasn't much she had wanted from him this afternoon. Just a few words alone, a chance to synchronize beforehand. After being married to him for fifteen years, Jackie still found something comforting in his solid presence—no matter how maddening the mere thought of him could be. If they could have exchanged a few words alone before hearing what the counselor had to say, it would have helped. It would have helped if they could have started from the same place, united and in control. Maybe they could have gotten through it together.

But it hadn't worked out that way, had it? The reality was, it never did anymore. Maybe it never had.

No, that was wrong: Luke had been a good husband, a caring father. It was just that his time was all spoken for. Not that he hadn't tried at first, just after they split, he had. He had known, as she had, that though their marriage was over, their responsibilities weren't. They still had a job to do: bringing up the children. And at least they agreed that it could only be done well if they did it together. They had been friends before they had been lovers, or so the story went. They could certainly stay friends afterward—for the children's sake.

Friendship notwithstanding, the escalating demands of his law practice (not to mention the distractions of moving in with young Isabel) had constricted his time. And of course Jackie was the first to get the brunt of that, which was of course better than Anna and Ben getting it. At least he still spared whatever time he had for them. Which was why he had shown up here at two-thirty on a weekday filled with work so important that he had left the children under Isabel's charge this morning. Jackie had to give him that. At least he had shown up.

But damn him anyway.

Jackie looked up from the squares of sidewalk and saw the brick front of the school just as the dismissal bell rang. Some of the other mothers were gathered at the school's front flagpole, busily engaged in gossip, and Jackie saw how their manner changed as she approached. She was happy to join in fund-raising for the school and to make costumes for the stage productions and to bake cookies when needed, but she had never been drawn in by the cords of whispered talk that bound so many mothers together. Jackie spent so much time at the school because of Ben and Anna. Not for her own entertainment. She knew the other mothers thought she was aloof, maybe even intimidating. Many of them had had careers as demanding as hers before their children came, but few of them maintained that discipline in their lives now. And Jackie did. She was no-nonsense.

Luke had of course pointed this out as one of her flaws. He called it her "unwillingness to share herself with anyone but the kids." His evidence was that they had lived in Nyack for a decade, and she had made only one friend, Colleen, a trust-fund artist who lived next door and painted watercolors of the Hudson in all the changing light of morning, noon, and evening, in high summer and slanted autumn and blunt winter. Jackie had not even tried to explain to him that Colleen was welcome in her life because she didn't intrude upon it. On a day here or there, Colleen might call across the lilac hedge and ask if Jackie was interested in a cup of sweetened mint tea. They would talk for an hour about, say, the kinds of sunflowers Monet grew, and then each would go back to her separate life. Colleen might show up to push Ben in the swing or to make Rose of Sharon dolls with Anna. But she was like nothing so much as the shade moving across the lawn on a long afternoon. She was quiet and cool and just there. She did not intrude upon the only society that Jackie cared to keep, which was that of her children.

The very efficient president of the PTA, who loved talking on the phone, was among the mothers gathered at the flagpole. As Jackie walked up, she asked Jackie about being in charge of the costume committee for the Thanksgiving pageant. And Jackie said, of course, and the two of them discussed what was being planned this year. But, all the same, Jackie was relieved to be released from the other mothers' polite chat by the bell. Kids came pouring out of the doors. Anna and Ben fell on her eagerly. Which was what she needed. She herded them back down the sidewalk, toward home.

Jackie was grateful that it was her night with them. The meeting with the counselor had unsettled her. Jackie was so busy blaming everyone else, and rightfully: Luke was paid three hundred dollars an hour to justify any sort of criminal behavior, so he certainly knew how to justify his own convenient new life. And Isabel clearly had no business dabbling in motherhood at the expense of Anna and Ben. But no matter how wrong Luke was and no matter how incompetent Isabel had proven herself to be, Jackie wasn't blameless either. She was guilty of her own feelings. That much was true.

But it was a beautiful day, a fact that had largely been lost on her until just now, until she had seen Ben running ahead of them through a shaft of sunlight that brought out blue shades in his dark hair. It was a day not to be wasted on self-pity, a day when the late-summer heat held ribbons of cool air that promised fall. The first aster bud had unfurled its fringed blossom today by the fence, and the Hudson reflected the most cobalt sky since springtime.

The three of them meandered home along the sidewalks that were bucked up on the roots of the old shade trees. Ben pocketed so many acorns that he bulged at the hips, and Anna told her mother a complicated account of a lunchroom scandal involving how Peter Bingley tried to get Jessie Tate to eat a cookie even though the cookie had peanut butter in it and peanut butter makes Jessie's throat swell shut and she could even die.

At home, Jackie and the children sat in the Adirondack chairs on the lawn and watched the river turn orange as the sun went down, and later while Jackie choreographed supper, Ben put on his magician's cape and shuffled cards, trying to perfect a new trick. Anna sat at the table sketching in pastels, a favorite pursuit recently, and Jackie thought she showed talent. There was something of Chagall's whimsy in her daughter's creations, and certainly the primitive beauty of Ludwig Bemelmans.

It was one of the finest gifts of motherhood, Jackie thought, seeing what your child made of the world around her, how she reinterpreted it. The first time Anna had drawn a stick family portrait, Jackie had been forced to turn away quickly so her daughter wouldn't see the tears that had welled into her

eyes. The biggest thing about the three people in
the crayon picture—Mommy, Daddy, and little
Anna—was the way they were smiling: big orange-
slice smiles. Jackie had been stunned to see her
child's evocation of happiness, to see the confirma-
tion that it was real and part of her life.

But Anna's creativity had a darker side now,
didn't it? And Jackie could recognize that, too, plain
as orange-slice smiles. Now, her daughter was making up tales at school, and they were tales that confirmed something about Anna's deepest heart. They
were tales that confirmed what it was Anna wished
to be but could never make happen on her own. Except through feats of make-believe. Except through
lying.

As she brought in the plates to set the table,
Jackie mentioned to Anna what the counselor had
told them today.

"I didn't say that," Anna said, without looking
up from her picture. "Why would I say that you and
Daddy are getting back together?"

Jackie had never known Anna to fib to her face
before, and it surprised her, the capacity for deceit
in her own child. Maybe she had miscalculated how
deeply her children had been affected by the divorce
and its aftermath. She had thought she could stand
between them and the trouble—a barrier against the
worst of it. If she didn't show her pain, the children
might not recognize their own or how deeply it
went. It was wrong-headed. Jackie said, "Daddy and
I were thinking that sometimes people tell stories.
About what they wish would happen."

"I don't want that to happen. Why would I want

that to happen?" Anna chose a blue piece of chalk and began sweeping away at the background.

Ben extended a deck of cards to Jackie. "Pick a card. Any card." He was using his inflated magician's voice.

She picked a card, but she spoke to Anna. "Maybe you're upset that Isabel moved in."

"I'm not upset. I'm not gonna get myself upset over *her*." She still did not look up from her work.

"Well, look . . ." she said to Anna.

Ben said, "Okay, tear it in half."

Jackie glanced down at the card she had chosen from his deck and tore it in half, even as she was still trying to talk to Anna. "If the . . ."

Ben interrupted. "Again."

Jackie tore the card in quarters. "If the . . ."

Ben insisted, "Again." Jackie shot him a funny look but kept tearing.

Anna looked up now, straight at her brother. "Ben," she said. "Get lost."

Jackie finished tearing the card into little pieces, and Ben took the pieces of card and folded them into a small stack of colored envelopes, even as Jackie turned back to her daughter, "As I was saying . . . if the truth is you don't feel like talking about this right now, that's fine."

Anna almost rolled her eyes.

"But don't look me in the face and lie to me." Jackie sat down in the chair next to Anna's, held her eye. This was too horrible, her daughter's dispassion. Her coolness. Jackie maintained a light tone, though, tried to tease something out of her daughter. She said, "'Cause there are only so many lies you're allowed to tell before it starts showing up on your face. And you wind up looking like . . ."

Jackie got up to get the glasses.

"Like who?" Anna asked, curious now, looking over her shoulder as Jackie opened the cupboard.

Jackie joked, "Well, he's not president anymore, so why be petty?"

Ben waved his wand over the folded papers, putting a spell over it. "Abracadabra, ala-kazam, ala-kazoo . . ."

Anna looked at Jackie. Her expression was suddenly honest, open, as though she had thrown open the shutters. "I'm sorry I said it. It just slipped out. I guess sometimes I just . . . Sometimes I do wish you and Dad would . . . You know . . ."

Jackie reached for her. "I know," she said. And she did.

"Figured if maybe I said it out loud . . . maybe it would come true."

Ben was working over his cards intently, and Jackie pulled Anna close so that she could hear her daughter when she said, softly and with such palpable dread, "What happens when he loves Isabel more than us?"

Jackie said, "That will never happen."

"Never say never," Anna said glumly, using Jackie's own words against her. Jackie couldn't think of how to answer that, her own wisdom applied in a way that would hurt the ones she loved the most. Never say never.

"Poof," Ben cried. "I've restored your card." Tapping the pile of colorful envelopes with his wand, he reopened them. He handed her the king of diamonds.

Jackie looked at it, then back up at him. "That's not my card."

"Huh?"

"I had the seven of clubs."

Ben's face stretched in shock, each feature stark. "No way."

"Way."

Anna said, "Is Daddy mad at me, too?" The worry knitted her eyebrows together.

"Honey, nobody's mad. We just want to talk about it."

"Pick a card. Any card." Ben extended the cards to Jackie, fanned out.

She picked one and told her daughter, "Daddy and I will always be there."

Anna said, "It's not fair to say always."

Jackie smiled, as much to herself as to Anna, and it was a weak smile, spurred by a sense of the irony in this moment. She smiled because they absorbed you, your children, whether they gave frequent signs of it or not. They absorbed everything you thought and felt and dreamed, and then they turned it back on you: showed you yourself in the most revealing mirror. "This is one time when always is always," she assured her daughter.

But her smile must not have been all that convincing. Her own feelings must have shown through because Ben turned his magic on her suddenly. "Poof," he said, ostentatiously striking Jackie with his wand. Too hard, the little beast. It hurt. "Poof," he announced. "You're happy now."

Poof. If only it were that easy, she thought, as she grabbed hold of him and pulled him close and tickled him until he laughed wildly and bucked to be free. The pink of his cheeks grew red. He hiccuped mirth. His heartbeat pulsed in his temple. And then she acknowledged that maybe it was that easy. Sometimes. Now. This minute. Poof: She was happy.

ISABEL

It was the best hour of the day, the hour when she got to stop at the Korean on Houston and buy sunflowers and then turn the corner on Greene, where she could look up at the curved loft windows and see the lights on and know that Luke was home already. It was the hour when the thought that had come around in her mind all day—looping through the concentration that commandeered the computer program and set the aperture on the Leica—got proved. It was the hour when she got to prove it to herself: Finally, she had someone to come home to.

Isabel had not minded living alone. After work, if she hadn't worked until midnight, she had gone to her apartment and punched the button on her answering machine, and it had given her the choices for the evening. There might be a screening in Tribeca with Matt, or a gallery opening with Glory, or maybe Guy would want to have sushi. Failing any of that, she always had a table waiting in Antoine's around the corner. It was heavy Italian food, but Antoine claimed to love her and would make anything fat-free. "For you, my Isabella," he would say, "I will wring the fat right from it." (So he promised; sometimes she had her suspicions.) Anyway, she loved eating at Antoine's in the back booth with a bottle of Pinot Grigio icing next to her elbow, and the waiters paying every bit as much attention to her as her grandmother Celie would have. It was like being home. Like being six and nothing had gone wrong yet and supper was almost ready.

Now, she had a real home. With Luke. His little black-pepper hair shavings were reliably in the bathroom basin in the morning, and in the dark if she woke and thought too much about what it was possible to lose in life, she could slide her foot over and touch his for comfort, and if it rained on Saturday night and the taxis started bunching up and honking down on the street, she and Luke could lie on their couch, twined together, and turn up the music until it obliterated every sound but the way the blood beat in her ears when he kissed her.

Who would have thought that it would happen to her, that kind of love? She herself had doubted it. She had thought she might go on forever having sex in the rooftop garden of her building with the hockey player who lived down the hall. Or having sex in the shower with the Parisian who came to town every other month and who always called and always made her laugh. Or having sex on the kitchen floor with Charley, who had been her first French kiss in junior high school and who still made her feel like that awkward twelve-year-old when he got up and pulled on his pants and left. She had thought she might even learn to be satisfied with something like that, with one of those guys even. She thought one of those relationships might be love. For all she knew.

She had not even known for certain that she

could be happy with one guy, with familiarity and expectation and responsiblity. But that had been before she met Luke. It had happened in Dean & De-Luca's, which she hated because it was all food snobs in there, people who sampled the olive oil on the counter and claimed to detect a difference between the pale yellow one and the deep green kind. For her, food was fuel. She only cared if it was easy. Also, the fewer the fat grams the better. Dean & DeLuca's was not for her; it was for people who cared.

But the store was on the way home from a dawn shoot, and she was ravenous and too spent to think of anything but going home and collapsing. So she had gone in to buy an apple—microwave popcorn, Häagen-Dazs chocolate sorbet, and a piece of fruit were standard fare on days that started too early and went on too long—and there were too many apples to choose from. She had been standing there with a green one in her hand, looking at one with red that edged into green and not being able to decide, and some man had said, "What do you want from it?"

Was he talking to her? She had looked up, and there had been this man who could throw a long shadow. He was frankly balding and straight through the shoulders, and he would have been not her type at all—too old—except he had this grin that made him look maybe six. And blue eyes, pure clear navy blue eyes that pierced right through her skin, right to the center of her.

He was smiling when he asked her again, "What do you want from it?"

"Want from it?"

He nodded at the apple she was weighing in the

palm of her hand. "If you want to make apple crisp, you can't beat this. It cooks down to velvet. Melts on your tongue." He held up a little apple with green blushing to red. "And if you want it for an apple tart, you want this because it slices beautifully and stays firm even when you bake it and caramelize it under the sugar." The one he held up was bright green. "Or if you want it for a Waldorf . . ."

"For eating," she said sharply. Food snob alert. "Out of my hand."

"Do you prefer sweet or tart? Do you want it to crunch or be soft?"

"I don't know."

He laughed. "Well, you have to know what you want, or you're never going to get it."

That was the moment. She swore it was that fast, nothing but the time it took to relay the wisdom of apples and every other thing in life: *You have to know what you want, or you're not going to get it.* She knew she wanted him then, food snob or not. And she had got him. He belonged to her. To her.

Luke called to her from the kitchen when she came in the front door of the loft. She could smell the meal he was preparing. The way he cared about food was a way of caring about her, she had found. The care he took was for her, and she found this amazing. The thought of it went through her, warm as wine. And after she had changed into a henley and some drawstring pants, she sat on the kitchen counter and watched him chop the herbs and onions. As long a day as he had put in, he was still willing to do this for her—and he seemed truly to enjoy it.

Sipping a glass of chardonnay, she tried to pay attention to more than just the way the muscles worked under his skin when he rocked the knife back and forth, mincing garlic. Poor man, he was still laboring under the assumption that she would someday become a cook herself, and he narrated his process for her even though she reminded him that it wasn't that she couldn't cook, it was only that she chose not to. He kept on like some kind of manly Julia Child, narrating every motion. Isabel thought it was adorable. "Fresh herbs, some basil, parsley, chicken stock. Then stir," he looked up to make sure she was watching. "Go on . . ."

She leaned over, took the spoon, began to stir. He looked down the counter, searching for something that wasn't where he had left it. "Where's the white wine?"

She swallowed a sip of it, toasted him with what was left in the glass. "Oh, you needed that?"

He threw her a look, one of his best ones. And she smiled back, tasted the sauce off her finger. "This is so good," she told him. "If you could make love this well, I'd marry you."

He hooked his arm around her and pulled her close and covered her mouth with his, kissing her deeply the way she loved. She could go down inside his kisses, get lost in them. They were like a door into him, and she could wander forever, never come back. And that's where they were going. They were going now . . .

The phone rang.

Isabel sighed, pulled away reluctantly, and put her hand out to answer it. "Hello?" Nothing. "Hello?" Someone hung up on the other end. Isabel hung up, too, turned back to Luke. But the moment was gone. He was back to the sauce.

"Oh," he said, "the Hanson-McAlpine trial's been postponed. Which means I have more work to do in Pittsburgh. Won't be back until Sunday—"

She twinged with disappointment, but feigned horror. "So I'll have to order in?"

"Well, we have the kids for the weekend. So I figured you guys might want to come with me . . ."

"To Pittsburgh," she blurted. "I love you. But I don't love you that much."

He grinned. "C'mon. We'll get a great hotel room. Take the kids to the zoo, a baseball game . . ."

"Never gonna happen. We'll be fine." At least she thought they would be fine. Of course they would be fine. They were ages seven and eleven. She was older than the two of them put together.

"Okay. Then maybe . . . while I'm gone . . . Maybe I'll hire in some help."

It took a minute for it to register, for it to sting as much as it was going to. It hurt. After how she had worked this morning. After how she had worked other mornings and afternoons and bedtimes. "For what?" she scoffed.

"Just a baby-sitter. I don't expect you to handle them yourself."

"*Can't* handle them myself is what you mean."

The phone rang again. Which was lucky for him. She answered. "Hello?"

Nothing.

"Who is this?" Isabel asked into the receiver.

Silence.

"Hello?"

A click. Dead air. Isabel slammed down the phone. But the frustration was not just for the prank caller but for the situation with Luke, his not trusting her with the kids. "You don't trust me to be alone with your kids," she accused him.

"I trust you. Of course I do. But . . ."

"But. But what?"

"I just don't think you should have to take care of them by yourself."

Sometimes she could hear the lawyer in him, working her his way with just the right angle. She resented it. "Luke," she said, "by keeping me apart from your kids . . . it's like telling them to keep hating me."

"They don't hate you." He was still stirring the sauce as if it would ruin without his complete concentration, as though it were some delicate French concoction and not some recipe he had come up with in law school to entertain Jackie when they were too poor for anything but cheap home cooking.

"Really?" Isabel challenged him, and she felt a pinch of self-loathing even as she did it. She loved him. She loved him so much. But why did there have to be these problems? Why did there have to be the kids? Ouch. She didn't mean that. But why couldn't he at least see the reality of the situation? How much she was trying—and how much they weren't? She said, "Look in their eyes. Look in your ex-wife's eyes."

"She's protective of her kids. What do you expect? It's complicated. You don't understand."

"Oh, right. So it's complicated for you and Jackie. For me it's pretty simple because I don't have kids."

It hurt him, her saying that. She could see it. She was going too far. She didn't want to hurt him. She just wanted to make him see that this wasn't easy for her either. It was simply the truth.

Up until she had fallen in love with Luke, her only contact with kids had been skirting their strollers on the street or winking at them in elevators. And she thought she was picking it up pretty damned fast. Considering.

Luke said, "I'm just trying to make this work . . . give you guys some time to get used to living together."

"So give us the time. We don't need a baby-sitter."

"Look, the kids are confused enough right now without . . ."

"Without what?" She had never pressed him this hard before.

"Without them not seeing their mother or father for two days. I don't want to make it any harder on them than it already is."

She lost it. She might not count as either a mother or as a father. But she did count. She told him: "I don't need another person in this family making me feel like an idiot. Your ex-wife's already doing a bang-up job, and I have to face it every Tuesday and Thursday and every other goddamn weekend. If you don't trust me with your kids, just say so."

She waited.

"No," he said. "I . . ."

"Then back off and give me a chance. Okay?"

The phone rang again, and this time she nearly ripped it off the wall, answering it. "What is your problem, asshole?" she said into the receiver.

"*You* are my problem," a voice said. A little

girl's voice. Anna's. And then she slammed down the phone.

Isabel looked at Luke. Holding the phone as evidence, she said quietly, "No, you're absolutely right. Your kids don't hate me. I'm just being paranoid."

He looked at her, then at the phone in her hand.

"Call your daughter," she said.

Taking it from her, he dialed his ex-wife's number, the number that had once been his, the number that would ring the phone in the lovely house on the Hudson where he had lived with his wife and kids, but not happily ever after. Isabel heard him talking to his daughter, soothing her, trying to send his comfort over the line, reach her some way. The sound of his voice made Isabel sad, completely sad. He tried so hard.

But so did she.

Isabel walked to the windows that looked south. The Twin Towers loomed, stark in the purest air the city had seen since springtime. Summer was starting to be worked away at, dissolved by the hard-approaching edge of autumn. She could see through the air again.

Wasn't Luke living happily ever after now? she thought. Or at least, wouldn't he be if . . . ? If only . . . But she stopped herself. They existed, his children. They were a fact. And he loved them. There was no such thing as a fairy-tale ending, not where divorce was concerned, and love that hadn't worked out, not when there were children caught in the middle.

Why couldn't they just love her? Or at least accept her?

What had she ever done but open her heart to them? From the beginning, she had been willing to adore them—not just to accept them—but to love them. She had known from the first night she and Luke had coffee together at Starbucks that he was a father. He had measured her with his eyes when he told her about Anna and Ben, and she had only smiled and said, "How lovely." Because it was. It was lovely for a man to acknowledge his children and also how he treasured them. It was lovely and just.

And she had not been lying to him several weeks later when their relationship had deepened past attraction and past the ravening lovemaking, when they had started to think of themselves as "us." She had not been lying or evading anything with him when he told her outright that the children were his responsibility and his joy, and they would be part of his life. Was she willing to share him with Anna and Ben?

Yes, she had told him then. Wholeheartedly yes. And she had been telling him yes in other ways ever since: by ignoring Anna's refusal to speak to her the afternoon they were introduced over frozen hot chocolate at Serendipity; by overlooking the fact that Ben refused to let her put a Band-Aid on his scuffed knee even though Luke had to log off the Internet to come do it; by enduring the way Luke's lioness ex-wife clawed her with every single glance. When she could, Isabel had volunteered to pick them up from school, to take them back to Nyack. She had snatched hours away from her work, and she had acted like it was no big deal. After all, she remembered how it was, being a child whose care

LUKE

Luke followed the kids along a cobbled path that led deeper into Central Park. Tomorrow, he had to leave for Pittsburgh, for the pain-in-the-ass Weis case. But today, he was stealing time away from the office, and like some kind of screwy Robin Hood, giving it to Anna and Ben. But sometimes a guy just knew when he had to do something for his kids. There weren't that many chances, with these two. They were like shuttlecocks, batted over the net that had gone up between his life and their mother's. Sometimes lately, it seemed like Isabel was that net. Jackie acted as though there had never been anything else wrong between them—before Isabel—as though there had never been nights that strained their vocal cords and their patience and their love, nights that had finally strained everything to breaking.

Luke told himself it would be better for the kids, in the end: the divorce. He believed that. It had been no way of growing up, confronted every day with the bitterness that had been like another person, or a whole crowd of people, living in the house in Nyack with them. At least now, Jackie could be happy—if she had it in her, and he really didn't know if she did anymore. In fact, he could hardly remember the woman who had learned to cook Szechuan with him and who stayed up late reading over his cases with him, the woman who liked to walk in the rain. Now, Jackie was so damned self-contained.

No, he didn't know about Jackie anymore. All he knew for sure was that *he* could be happy. Isabel had proven that he could be; he still owned that capacity. Anna and Ben wouldn't have their mother and him together maybe. But they would have their parents' individual happiness. They would have his at least, and with it, they would have days like this one in the park.

The new sailboat had been a good idea. He didn't want to be one of those guys who bought his kids off. Not like Kendrickson at the office who was all the time ordering some new toy from Hammacher Schlemmer and having it shipped to his ex-wife's house in the 'burbs. As if his kids cared that the trampoline had set him back a couple of thousand. As if that proved anything to them. But the sailboat was different. It had given the three of them an easy distraction—the good-natured quibbling over which boat to buy at F.A.O. Schwarz, the slow but eager walk through the park to the boat pond, their three heads bent over the operating instructions, which were partly in German. It had given them a way to get back to each other after everything had gotten crazy.

The other night, Jackie told him later, she had found Anna in her room with the cordless. She had been calling Luke and getting Isabel and hanging up. There had been the twin explosions then—the one in Nyack and the one in the kitchen in SoHo.

Of the two, Luke had felt better able to handle Isabel's. She was susceptible to his charms. Falling asleep that night, he had spooned her and whispered in her ear about all the ways he loved her, and before he knew it, she had rolled over and was showing him all the ways she loved him. And it was just what he needed in the middle of a trial, to stay up too late making love. But it was just what he needed.

His daughter was another matter. From the day he had first held her as an infant, from the first time she had wrapped her tiny fingers around his thumb, he had vowed to let nothing hurt her. His love for her was something fierce in him, and inarticulate. Any words he tried to attach to the feeling were lame. When Ben came along, it was no different. Luke's love for his children was simply his purpose, the most pure thing he had ever felt: Loving them burned in him like vodka knocked back, brilliant and sharp. It was what propelled him upward in his career, through exhaustion at their bedsides, through hours of peewee soccer. He wanted to protect Ben from all harm, to stand guard against his daughter ever being hurt.

And then he had hurt them himself. By leaving when he should have fought to stay. By leaving when he might still have found a way over or through or under Jackie's intractability. But he had gone and gone after something for himself finally, some life where he didn't have to negate himself but only expand and grow and surge ahead. Now he had it. And he couldn't help fearing that Anna, his little daughter, was paying the price.

Anna was upset at getting caught in the lie at school, certainly. But Jackie swore that it was more than that, and Jackie was rarely wrong when it came to her children. That much he had to give her. As their mother, she got vibrations off them that he had never been able to fathom—from the way they held their lips or from the smell of their hair or from the story they wanted read at bedtime. Who knew? But the night of the phone fiasco, she had crawled into bed with Anna and curled up to eat chocolate yogurt, and she had known just from that quiet time in the dark there, just the two of them, that there was more wrong than she could fix. Maybe, she had pointed out gravely, there was more wrong than Luke could fix.

But he had to try. And the only way he knew to try was to be there, to be with the kids.

He was waiting Anna out now, as they played in the water with the sailboat. He knew that she knew what she felt, and that she would get around to revealing it. She always had. She took after her mother in that way, for better or worse. And as the boat motored along the edge of the pond with Ben at the controls, she finally worked herself around to bringing it up. Luke was touched by her somewhat awkward attempt at nonchalance.

"How long are you gonna be out of town?" she asked.

"Sunday morning."

She fiddled with a weed. "I'm worried."

"About what?"

"About being alone. All weekend. With her." She looked up to see how he would react to this, and he kept his expression even and open to her. She had to know she could talk, that she could tell him anything—even if it was about Isabel. "What if she burns the place down?" she asked.

He smiled. It was a smile meant to reassure, not to scoff. "Just keep a fire extinguisher handy."

Anna smirked. "Why did she have to move in with you anyway?"

Here it was. He gathered himself and tried to measure out the words. "Well, because we love each other. And we want to share our life together."

Ben had come within range by then, and he spoke up. "But you already had a life. With Mommy," he pointed out.

How did you explain something so complex to a child? How did you explain that by luck of the draw you ended up in freshman English lit with a cute tough-minded redhead and by mid-semester you were relying on her for help with your Shakespeare paper and by the next semester you were sleeping together every time your roommate went to swim laps and before you knew it years had passed and you had graduated and moved in together and gotten married? And it was like nothing so much as rolling down a hill? How did you explain to your kids that love was as arbitrary as what classes you got freshman year at college and who was on the other side of the armrest? How did you explain that their being in the world at all was nothing but the accident of two lives rolling downhill together? You didn't.

You couldn't.

Luke said, "But we weren't getting along real well. It wasn't fair to you guys, us fighting all the time."

"I fight with Anna all the time. Does that mean I have to move out?"

Luke thought, *He's got the lawyer blood.* He said, "No, but you guys are brother and sister."

Anna jumped back in, "And you guys were husband and wife. Isn't that just as important?"

"Yes," Luke agreed, "it is." He tried to find the right words. "But men and women . . . when you get older . . . your relationships get more complicated. There are a lot of different feelings, and sometimes you lose some of those feelings."

"Like love," Anna offered with gravity. And he heard something of her mother in her again.

"Yeah. Sometimes."

"Did you fall out of love with Mommy?" she asked. It was hard for her to ask. He could tell it cost her by the way her nose got red. Whenever she was struggling with something, whether it was long division or the long division of her parents' hearts, her little nose flushed that way.

He tried to answer evenly, kindly, "Well, yeah. I guess maybe in one way. But it changed into a different kind of love. I still care about her. We're still friends . . ."

Ben looked at him. "Can you ever fall out of love with your kids?"

Luke's heart constricted inside him. "No," he said, bundling them both against his chest in one sudden motion. "That is impossible," he promised. He looked down into their faces to gauge whether they believed him. And they did.

He had waited all day for the two smiles he saw. All day. And maybe all week.

ISABEL

Isabel stared at the computer screen. But she was concentrating on something far more complicated than QuarkXPress. She twirled the silver rings on her finger. She rattled her bracelets. She ignored Cooper, who kept shooting her looks.

The word in her family was that she would never grow up. Isabel had been the last of the kids after all, the baby, and then with everything that happened when she was little, she got by with more than her brothers or sisters had. Grandma Celie had always said she was spoiled rotten to the core and would never outgrow it, although Grandma herself had been largely responsible for the spoiling. Probably it was true that she would never outgrow her childhood, Isabel thought. To this day, whenever she called her father he said, "Well, how's my little daughter?"

So, shouldn't she be able to use her outsize youthfulness to her advantage now? Shouldn't she be able to think like a kid?

Noodling at her computer, she worked on how to come at Ben and Anna from their own level. Luke had all but issued a challenge to her by not trusting her with them this weekend. And Isabel was still as susceptible to a challenge as she had been in third grade when Wheeler Channing said he could make one hundred baskets in a fifteen-minute recess, and she couldn't. Being a girl. So she had. Even if it did make her so dizzy that she upchucked behind the lilac bush.

Cooper kept scrutinizing her, the way he did. And finally he got tired of telepathy and asked her why she was zoned out, and she told him she was trying to think like a kid so she could relate to Luke's kids. Cooper got that all-knowing look on his face that told her to give it up, and she had said, "Shut up, and help me." To which he replied that he had a Visa card, a one-bedroom apartment, and a three-hundred-dollar pair of glasses, all of which disqualified him from thinking like a kid and anyway, it wasn't something that he wanted to revert to. "A kid," he told her, "can look at something he digs from his nose and wonder what it tastes like. I can't go there."

It was hard going there, Isabel had to admit. It was hard going Back There. She had her own grown-up acquisitions: a man, a car payment, an assistant to tend her Filofax, not to mention a rather financially demanding Armani habit. And it was a long way from there back to being so carefree that a good night was catching toads around the foundation of Johnny McKee's house. It was a long way back to the time when the jangle of the ice-cream truck could infuse a slow afternoon with excitement and a sense of mission: how to charm a dime out of Grandma's mad-money jar in time for a rocket pop. Where she was now was a long way from the nights when time stopped and she lay in bed and remembered the things that she could halfway forget when she was cannonballing into the public pool or sneaking raspberries off the neighbors' vines. Now was a long way from the nights when she was alone in the darkness and knew what it was to be helpless, to know that life was beyond her control and it took things away—people included—and she had no say at all, and the only comfort then was to stroke Old Matt between the ears and try to match her breathing to his snoring and to think that he had been around forever, that old dog, and so there was every reason to believe that he always would be.

And there it was: a dog. She loaded Cooper into the Land Rover with her, and they drove to the pound in Queens, even though he said the smell would make him sick (and he wasn't exaggerating). They brought home the most beautiful golden retriever puppy with bottomless eyes the color of melted Hershey's. The puppy trembled at Isabel's touch, loved her with his tongue. He was perfect.

That night, after Jackie had dropped off the kids and after Luke had eaten supper with them and then said good-bye for the weekend, Isabel had gone into her bedroom and brought out the puppy. He was a sweet guy, and she stood just outside the kitchen with him, taking her last minute of unshared nuzzling. She could hear Anna and Ben in there. They had been aloof since their father left for Pittsburgh, as if to say that they would be fine here going about their own business, just mind your own. Now, Ben was making a magical recipe. Isabel heard him reciting in his deep-register magician's cadence: "Two spoons of powdered lizard brains. Three pinches of crushed werewolf ears. One cup of vampire sweat.

"Check it out," he told his sister proudly. "Magic potion."

"It's cocoa."

"I put a spell on it. Whoever drinks it will go to sleep for a thousand years."

"Whatever," Anna said. "Spill any on my drawing, and you'll go to sleep for a thousand years."

Isabel set the puppy down behind the couch and went in to defuse the situation. Then she primed them for the unveiling of The Surprise. She herded them onto the couch and sat them side by side. "I've got a big surprise for you," she told them. "Close your eyes. Come on."

Ben closed his eyes. He could still be bossed around, especially with the bait of a reward. But of course Anna had to sigh and flaunt her reluctance before closing her own.

Isabel stooped behind the couch and lifted the puppy. She sat him between the two kids. "Okay. Open."

The kids opened their eyes. Ben flushed with happiness and pulled it onto his lap as if by reflex. Even Anna couldn't disguise her true feeling, which looked to be delight. Immediately, though, she put on a frown. She made a big production of putting on a frown and leaning away from her brother and the pup.

"Well?" Isabel asked, climbing up on the back of the couch and looking down at them. "What do you think?"

"Will he eat my bunny?" Ben asked, although

Isabel thought from the way he was making out with the puppy, the bunny would have to take its chances.

"Puppies don't eat bunnies," she assured him.

Ben was rubbing noses with the retriever, and still Anna just sat bunched into her corner, skeptical. Isabel tried to draw her into the circle, "Anna?"

Anna shrugged coolly. "I'm allergic to dogs."

"Your father never said anything about that. He said you love dogs." (What Luke *had* said, when he had met the puppy in the privacy of their bedroom earlier, was, "You do know you'll have to peel the smiles off of them when they get ahold of this guy?")

"He doesn't know anything about me," Anna said caustically. "He's never around."

Isabel felt her adrenaline spike. Of course. Of course the little brat would do this, reject any attempt to make peace, to make progress. And it was one thing to direct it at Isabel. That was one thing. But directing it at her father, at Luke, that was another thing entirely. And it was too far.

Oh, well, it wouldn't do anybody any good to indulge Anna's sullen temper. Instead Isabel tried to change the topic, "The puppy needs a name. Any ideas?"

"Isabel," Anna suggested bluntly.

"Pardon?"

"He kinda smells like you. And I'm allergic to you, too. Fits perfectly."

Isabel wanted to let her temper loose. But she didn't. She was the adult here, and no matter how much she was trying to think like a child, she had to react with maturity. So she reached out to Anna and said, "Let's not fight . . ."

Anna lurched away and spat, "Don't touch me. I'm allergic to you, remember?" She began to make a show of sneezing and furiously scratching even as she gathered her drawing and pastels. As she hurried out of the room, she barked: "I have to work on my art project. Don't follow me. I can put myself to bed."

For a beat, Isabel didn't follow. She watched Ben playing absorbedly with the puppy. He was gone where only seven-year-olds can go with a puppy.

When she heard the music blare on in Anna's room, Isabel couldn't ignore the tantrum anymore. She barged in. It wouldn't be right to let the girl get away with this. If she didn't want to play nicely, Isabel wouldn't play. She would act her own age, which trumped Anna's. "Listen, young lady . . ." the sound of that awful phrase rang in her ears and made her pause long enough to hear the distinctive pulse of familiar music coming out of the stereo. "Is this Pearl Jam?" she asked Anna.

Anna nodded.

"First record?"

"Second."

Isabel listened for a second. There was a reason that music worked—because it worked its way inside you, got under your skin. But she remembered what she had come for, which was scolding Anna. She turned stern, tried to get her point across. "Anyway. Let's get something clear."

"I don't have to listen to you. You're not my mother."

"Thank God for that," Isabel said, slamming the door behind her on the way out.

Which was not very grown-up, she realized, and so she went back in. She hadn't been so angry that she hadn't noticed the pain that flashed across Anna's face when she said that. It was gratuitous. It was immature of Isabel to have said it.

"What I meant," she explained to Anna, "and perhaps I didn't say it well, was that you have a great mom. You don't need another one. But I would like to be treated with some respect when you're at this house . . ."

"This is my daddy's house."

"This is my house, too." Firmly.

"And this is my room," Anna said viciously. "So get out."

Isabel paused. If she had ever spoken to an adult in that tone when she was a kid, she would have been picked up by the ears and dangled out the highest window until she begged for mercy. But what could Isabel do? What could she do but swallow her frustration and close the door on the way out. Anna was a desperately unhappy child. But she was not Isabel's desperately unhappy child. She was just Isabel's problem.

After that, the exhaustion settled over her. Isabel had spent her energies all day with the goal of pleasing them, of getting through to them. And she had failed.

Failure wasn't something she understood, and it felt heavier to her than exhaustion. As a photographer, she threw herself into the task. She worked long hours and hard. But she just had this innate sense of how to transform the ordinary into the extraordinary. She knew how to bend all the elements—lens, natural light, synched flashes, computer wizardry—to her purpose. Work never wore her out so much as it exhilarated her. It wasn't like this. This was more like a bad date, one of those really bad ones during which she used to be overwhelmed by an insatiable need to sleep, a need to just escape into some dream where the date couldn't follow. These kids were like a bad date.

She had done her best—only to have it hurled back in her face as not good enough. Sure, Ben liked the puppy, but it didn't appear to warm him any toward her. When it was time for bed, he brought along the cup of cocoa, which she happened to know was specially brewed to make her sleep for a thousand years. Even though he didn't know she knew.

It didn't seem like such a bad option, just now, sleeping a thousand years. Sleep asked for no compromises: When she was in her bed and under her consciousness, she could have everything her way, pure and undiluted by the truth. Her brother used to call her a long-distance sleeper. Her grandma Celie said Isabel had an ON switch and an OFF switch, nothing in between. The whole family laughed about it. But, the truth of it was, she desperately loved to sleep. She loved to dream. She needed it. Especially when she was six and seven and eight. And especially now, when again she could not make everything all right just by smiling and working hard. When it wasn't enough, just being Isabel.

Ben wanted *The Stinky Cheese Man* for his bedtime book. And she tried to read, but there was a drag on her voice that didn't quite muster the vigor of the story: "Run, run as fast as you can, you can't catch me, I'm the Stinky Cheese Man."

Ben said, "Aren't you going to drink your cocoa? I made it *especially* for you."

She took a big sip to please him, a big old ostentatious sip. He watched excitedly, waiting for her to tumble into slumber and not wake up again in his lifetime. (She was half-waiting for it, too, hoping.) Still, he wasn't giving up on having his story read, either. So she kept going, skipping a bit here and there, then skipping whole pages while reading a hundred miles an hour, desperate for the end, for her bed, desperate for sleep so deep that she would utterly forget she had all of tomorrow to endure with these two, and all of the next day. Alone. Without Luke. She yawned helplessly. Maybe his cocoa potion was working on her after all. "A little boy looked up, sniffed the air . . ."

"No, you're cheating," Ben said. "You skipped the part about the cow."

"It's bedtime. We'll finish in the morning."

Seven-year-olds have rules, and Ben meant to enforce his. "No," he said with great authority. "Now we have to start from the beginning, and you have to read the whole thing. I can't sleep otherwise." His eyes were glued to her, inflexible.

The little tyrant. She lay down next to him, yawned again, and flipped the pages back. Reluctantly, she began again from page one. "Once upon a time, there was a little old woman, and a little old man . . ."

". . . who lived together in a little old house," Ben continued from memory.

"That's nice, Ben," she told him. "You're onto

something there. Go on." She laid her head down to listen until he read himself to sleep. Only she fell first, felt herself sliding down into the depths and not being able to stop, having no wish to stop, even when the little boy nudged her, then poked. She slid farther down but not far enough because still she dreamed about them, those two kids. In her dream, Ben was crowing in triumph to his sister: "I killed her. I killed her. I killed her!"

JACKIE

Every mother longed for it—just some time to herself. Staring out the kitchen window, Jackie remembered that when Anna was a very curious five-year-old and Ben was an infant, she had ached for quiet and slow hours. She had longed for Jane Austen's company and to drink a cup of tea while it was still hot enough to need blowing on. So when she and Luke had divvied up their custody of the children, she had soothed herself with the promise of just such solitude. Even at the time, she knew she was just putting a nicer spin on reality. She knew she was just trying to make it seem like time away from her children was something she could live with, even enjoy.

But she wasn't that kind of mother, really. She hadn't driven Luke out of their marriage by being the kind of mother who welcomed someone else taking charge of her little ones. She had driven him away by not being able to relinquish them to anyone else. And this was the result: Now, she had to.

She didn't admire who she had become, someone who holed up all weekend while the children were away and worked long numbing hours, freelance editing a coffee-table book that wouldn't change anybody's life. The book would become a useless object, gathering dust. Jackie did not admire uselessness, and so she did not admire the image she had of herself this instant: standing at her kitchen window and watering the pot of violas and washing her own teacup, doing anything to pretend that she wasn't watching the road for another woman to bring her children home to her.

Divorce wasn't something Jackie had wanted. She had gone into her marriage with nothing less than Forever as her goal. Her own parents had split up after twenty-three years together, split just when their daughter was eighteen and old enough to analyze why it happened. And in her mind it happened because of laziness, something she never allowed herself after that. In college, she was summa cum laude. She was the first in her class to nail a post-graduate job—so what that it was making a salary of only twelve-thousand dollars in the subrights department of a publishing house? It was the subrights department of a publishing house that had three Nobel laureates on its authors' list. Incrementally, she moved from editorial assistant to assistant editor to editor. She moved over to Random House and got a very nice salary, and she acquired a book that made the best-seller list the same year she married Luke.

She remembered the first time she had seen him. It was freshman year at college in an English lit lecture hall, and he was late, and there was only the seat next to her available. Dropping into it, he had grinned and nodded. And she had forced herself to respond with half a smile. But all through class, she had been aware of him. His skin smelled like woodsmoke. The hair of his arms brushed along hers on the shared armrest, and it raised gooseflesh. For her, it was instant infatuation.

And she probably would have gotten over it soon enough. Only he lived in a neighboring dorm and needed help with Shakespeare, which should have been a red light. But most of all, he was a break from being Jackie Carson Herself. Luke wasn't like she was. Not at all. He hadn't cared so much about learning as he had about experiencing what he could do, what he had the power to do. He had an athletic curiosity: He jogged five miles in the dusk of dawn; he played tennis ferociously; he biked fifty miles over a weekend. His blood really worked in his body.

His blood called to hers. She kept up with her studies (or ahead of them), stayed long hours in a cubby at the library, got up at dawn to read over her notes one last time before an exam. But she released the pressure of making the grades by making love with Luke. He didn't engage the deeper parts of her, the sinew of her intellect and heart that she required for Accomplishment. He engaged only her flesh—and completely. He was the first for her (and the only until a brief, regrettable attempt at romance three months after the divorce was final), and she had acknowledged to herself that she loved the swell of his biceps and the small of his limber back and the skeins of his hair between her fingers, she had loved all these parts of him, before she had ever thought of loving him.

They were together for years before she loved him in the way that she eventually came to believe was truly love. They had been lovers all through college and had moved to New York after college and shared an apartment. And still it wasn't what it would become. It was merely splitting the rent, the burden of Starting Out in Real Life. It wasn't love— not until the night of her friend Karen's wedding when Luke had held Jackie's hand in the cab on the way home, and said, "Let's do it." And when she had asked, "What?" he had said, "Get married." Everything changed then. It changed inside her. It was his willingness to commit that made her love him finally. Because by then she knew enough of him to know that once he committed, he was powerful.

For all his lackluster performance in college scholastically, he had emerged at graduation with a sense of himself that had been honed in races and matches and bodily contests. He had fight in him, a sharp calculating mind. He scored extremely high on the law school entrance exam and approached his legal studies as she had never seen him approach anything but physical competitions. He muscled his way through with honors, and afterward he landed resoundingly in one of New York's top firms. His athlete's agility informed his work. He was a tough and tenacious lawyer.

He had become a tender husband. And Jackie, too, had tackled marriage the same way she had tackled her career. And that might have worked. Together, they seemed to thrive. Their long hours at work only made them happier to see each other at the day's end. They took weekend trips to Montauk and long walks in the rain to eat Vietnamese on a street far south of their apartment. He weighed in with her on his work, and she consulted him about contracts. They stayed up late talking about fine points, arguing them until they got so riled up they could only defuse it with sex. Four years into their marriage, they still held hands in public.

Then Anna was born.

Standing at the sink, Jackie cupped water in her hands and patted her face with it. Who knew what made a marriage dissolve? If she had known at eighteen, judging her parents, she no longer claimed any certainty. It wasn't laziness, that much she could say. She had tried. Luke had tried. They had both worked, but after a while it just became clear that they were working against each other. And finally what she wanted most was exactly what she could never have.

Jackie looked at the clock again. Isabel and the children were thirty-nine minutes overdue, and she had no idea whether to be sick with worry—who knew if Isabel could drive safely in that kind of insane traffic—or whether to be furious that the simplest things couldn't be accomplished when that woman was involved.

Between these two divergent emotions, it was a simple choice when she finally saw Isabel's Land Rover pull into the driveway and stop.

Jackie started breakfast. At least the children would get a decent meal before she took them to school. Not everything was ruined for them because their father's lover either couldn't tell time—or couldn't respect it.

Isabel walked into the kitchen. Jackie could hear the children in the entrance hall, kicking off their shoes, squabbling.

Jackie said to Isabel, "How do you hold down a

job? It's seven-ten. You were supposed to be here at six-thirty. She's missed her Groom and Ride."

Isabel looked surprised. She began digging in her purse. "I got it right here. This is Monday. Her riding lesson is on Tuesdays . . ." Her voice took on a tinge of defiance, the defiance of being right.

Only she wasn't right. Jackie walked to the refrigerator where she had a neatly arranged system of Post-its. The schedule was outlined in careful detail. She pointed for emphasis. "Every Tuesday except the third Tuesday of the month when it's switched to Monday except in November when she rides on Thursday. It's not that hard. Didn't you have a mother?"

Isabel flinched, but said only, "Could I get a cup of coffee?"

"We don't have any coffee."

"What is this? The Betty Ford Center?"

As Anna came through the kitchen on her way upstairs, Jackie asked her, "Hi, baby, how was your weekend . . . ?"

But Anna had already rushed past her and up the stairs, obviously upset.

Jackie slapped a look on Isabel. "What happened with Anna? What did you do?"

Isabel looked like she could bite. "Maybe you could back off just a little bit . . ."

"What happened?"

Isabel looked sheepish. "Luke was in the shower this morning, and Anna sort of walked in without knocking," Isabel admitted.

Jackie pressed. "I'm sure that didn't upset her. Everyone in our family takes showers."

"I was in there with him."

Now Jackie flinched. It was involuntary. Luke had known what a lock was when he lived here. Before he lost his good sense over Isabel. She asked, "Did you or Luke talk to her about it afterward?"

"No," Isabel confessed. "I thought it might be uncomfortable for her . . ."

"You mean for you," Jackie fired back. Something close to rage was moving across every nerve. She could feel it in her vocal cords. "An eleven-year-old girl is coping with the fact that her father is never coming back to live with his family. She sees her father naked with another woman for the first time. And you think it's best for her if everyone pretends it didn't happen?"

Isabel seemed to expand in the room. "I'm sick of your imperious bullshit. I never said I was June Fucking Cleaver. If every time life hits her in the face you want to have a twelve-hour talk every third Tuesday of the month, go ahead. I have a life."

"And I don't?" Jackie asked. "Why? Because I have children? The problem is you're too self-involved to ever be a mother."

"I never said I wanted to be a mother."

"Now you're thinking rationally."

Isabel's face was solid around her anger. She said, "Maybe the problem is your daughter. Maybe she's a spoiled wise-ass little brat."

"Get out of my house."

"But it's not on the schedule," Isabel said, flipping a finger at the fridge Post-its. She locked eyes with Jackie. Then she left the house.

All the air seemed to follow her, and Jackie had to stand with both hands on the counter and try to breathe, try to pull in enough air so that she could go take care of the children. So that she could go braid Anna's hair and double-knot Ben's sneakers and try to say the words that were the answers to the questions that they couldn't even ask. So that she could go to them and do the little things that did not keep them one bit safer—but only made them feel safe. And made her feel that she was doing all she could. She tried to find enough air to breathe so that she could go upstairs to her children and forget *Sense and Sensibility* on her nightstand and the elastic hours of Sunday when time hung around her like fog, and wouldn't lift.

ISABEL

She wished she could blame it on the light. Really, the light was her boss that day, and she was answering to it. But Isabel knew it was no excuse. How many times had Luke told her about the Murphy's Law of kids vs. work?

It had started out as a good deed. The kids had a school holiday, and Luke had planned to take them to Coney Island but had gotten called away at the very last minute because one of his clients had been subpoenaed by the special prosecutor in Washington. Isabel had simply volunteered to let the kids come along with her—so they wouldn't have to wait out Luke's absence with that baby-sitter they hated who had sixteen moles on her face. It had seemed like such a perfect solution.

But that damned beautiful light . . .

Amateurs thought that a sunny day was perfect for photography, but professionals knew that a high gauze of clouds was better. Sheer clouds were a natural form of filter, softening shadows, making features appear as they truly were, undistorted by contrast. And that was what Isabel had going for her, that serendipity of weather and purpose: a morning photo shoot in Central Park with a screen of clouds.

The perfect light was irresistible to her, and she was immersed in it, lost in her work. To be honest, she did not even see the ridiculous scene beyond her lens. She saw the light on the faces, how it carved out their shapes against the castle walls. Though everyone around her was focused on how the guy dressed like a prince should hold his arm, how he should angle his leg so he appeared to be climbing Rapunzel's crazy-long hair, Isabel was busy working with the light.

Behind her, the kids were waiting on the ramparts. They had been bored the last time she remembered to check on them. She had appeased them with ice cream. Funny her, she had thought they might get a charge out of being on a photo shoot with her, and not just any photo shoot, but one in which two grown-ups were dressed up like fairytale characters. But the only comment either of them had made was when Ben said he thought it would be "way cooler if Rapunzel's hair came outta her armpits." To which his big sister had replied, "Sick."

So much for giving the kids a thrill.

Isabel looked up at the sky. She was afraid a front was going to come through and change the shooting conditions before she wrapped it up. If she pushed everybody through lunch, though, she was pretty sure she could nab everything before the weather thwarted her. And then they'd all be done early. But when she called out this order to the crew, she heard a cry of protest.

From Anna.

"Come on," the girl whined. "It's been five hours. We're hungry."

Isabel's mind flipped through her options: how to entertain them when she wasn't free to entertain them? She tossed them her wallet and told them to buy themselves another couple of Fudgsicles, and that was the last thought she tossed in their direction until she had outlasted the crew's impatience and captured the perfect confluence of light and action.

From this angle and that. From above, from below. *Voilà*, there it was. In the can. Perfect.

Then she looked around for the kids. Anna was asleep on a bench with the remains of Ben's ice cream melting beside her. "Lunchtime, Sleeping Beauty," Isabel told her.

Anna sat up groggily.

"Where's your brother? In the bathroom?"

"I don't know."

Isabel scanned the area. He wasn't on any of the ball fields. He wasn't poking around in the weeds by the pond, and as far as she could tell, squinting through the trees, he wasn't climbing any of the playground equipment. She felt the blood leave her face. She felt Anna watching her. Panic got her around the throat. "Ben!" she screamed. "Ben!"

No answer.

She whirled and ran toward the castle. Maybe he was hiding in one of its crannies: the vanishing-magician trick. Anna stayed on her heels, calling, too. "What if he's kidnapped?" she asked Isabel when they got to the front entrance.

"He's not kidnapped," Isabel said, praying he wasn't kidnapped, praying, praying. "He's . . . he's just hiding. He's just . . ."

Her thought broke off. "Ben," she cried, grabbing for Anna's hand so she wouldn't lose her, too, so she wouldn't lose both Luke's children in one thoughtless, stupid hour.

Anna slapped her away. "Don't touch me," she said. "You bring bad luck."

Isabel was starting to believe just that. She wanted to collapse and cry. But she forced herself into the castle. She called up the winding staircase, so that her voice echoed eerily back down to her. Ben's did not follow.

She started up, Anna trailing her.

Isabel stopped and called again. This time, she heard whimpering from farther up. It urged her on. "Ben," she called, "we're here."

They broke out onto the top floor of the castle, back out into the perfect light of day. But there was no Ben. There was only the golden retriever puppy, whimpering, lost. No Ben.

Anna said, "He's gone forever."

Isabel felt dizzy. She felt as though she would never draw another breath, as though she did not deserve ever to draw another. She leaned against the wall, looking over the side, down over the treacherous rocky cliffs below. No Ben. She looked out across the great wild stretches of the park, tried to see the color of his shirt. No Ben.

She screamed his name.

Isabel started running. There were woods and rocks and the lake. Oh, God, the lake . . . She headed toward the wildest part of the park, where a boy could get lost in the woods or fall off a rock into water. She ran. It was only Anna's voice, falling behind her, that pulled her to a stop.

Anna caught up with her, flushed and panting.

"Shouldn't we call the police?" the girl asked her. Even Anna was too afraid to be nasty now. She reached for Isabel's hand. "Shouldn't we?"

The police? Isabel thought. She couldn't. She couldn't admit that it was that bad. He had just wandered off. You didn't call the police for a kid who had probably just taken a notion to go exploring. You didn't bother the authorities over something like that, did you?

Anna looked at her intently. Isabel could see the fear in the girl's eyes. It was a real thing.

"Luke," Isabel said, the idea striking her suddenly. If she had to call someone, let it be Luke. "We'll call your dad."

Luke didn't answer his cell phone. She beeped him with the emergency code and kept walking. Anna struggled to keep up and kept reaching for Isabel's hand whenever her stride outstetched Anna's own eleven-year-old attempt. "Ben," they called in unison. "Benjamin."

Isabel's phone throbbed, and she closed her eyes and put it to her ear. Her hands where shaking. "Luke?" she asked.

"Isabel, what's wrong?"

"It's Ben," she said. "He wandered away from the set. I was working. I didn't watch him enough, and now, he's gone."

"Have you looked in the trees?" Luke said, sort of chuckling. "He's a climber, you know." Isabel could tell that he thought it was another of Ben's pranks on her. She could tell that Luke thought she was merely the butt of another joke.

"Luke," she said, managed to say because her

throat was closing on her, swollen with fear, "I think you need to call the police. I can't find him."

"Where did you last see him?" His voice was taut now, stretching toward her own realization.

"Outside the castle," she said.

"Okay." He hung up.

Anna said, "Is he calling?"

Isabel nodded.

"Ben," Anna yelled.

"Ben," Isabel echoed.

Anyone looking at them would have thought they were standing in the middle of the path screaming at each other. And maybe they were. Anna surely blamed her. And Isabel couldn't help but blame Anna a little for having dozed off. She was supposed to be such a responsible kid.

Together, they turned and walked deeper into the trees. Anna looked up into the limbs. Isabel looked behind rocks. "This isn't funny," she yelled. That was for Ben's benefit. Or for whoever had Ben. Or for whoever had let this happen. It was for Isabel herself. "This isn't funny."

Anna's face was red, Isabel noticed finally. She could feel her own heart pounding and the way it seared her lungs to inhale. Isabel could tell the girl was hurting for breath, worse than she herself was certainly. She reached for Anna's hand, pulled her to a stop. They stood together and heaved to breathe. It was the last thing Isabel wanted to do: stop. But she was afraid for Anna.

"You okay?" she asked finally.

Anna nodded. "Ben," she croaked to the trees and boulders and winding paths.

Isabel's phone throbbed. "Yes?" she answered.

It was Luke. "The police are on the way."

"Okay."

"Where are you?"

She didn't know for sure. What did they call this part of the park? It was the tangled part. "I'm headed for the lake," she said.

"You need to start over toward the east side, Isabel. You need to get to the station house. You'll do them more good telling what Ben was wearing, what he looks like. I'm headed there now myself. As soon as I call Jackie."

That thought stopped her. She actually felt it run down her spine and twist in her stomach: *Oh, not Jackie. Of course, Jackie.* "Oh," she said aloud, that's all.

"I have to," he said. "She's his mother."

Of course she is, Isabel thought, *and Jackie would not have lost him. Jackie would not have let him out of her sight.* Jackie was right, right, right: Isabel was all wrong. And this proved it. It proved it to Jackie and to Luke. It proved it to Isabel.

She had left the children alone in Central Park. That's what it boiled down to—that hard truth? She had left two children alone in the park, while she was off waltzing with the goddamn light of day? What had she expected? If Luke had told her once, he had told her a dozen times: The trick with kids is anticipation. You look ahead, try to anticipate what will go wrong, and then you head it off. Any idiot could have seen what danger lay ahead if you left a couple of kids alone on a park bench. Any idiot.

But not Isabel.

"I'll call you back," Luke said. "Start heading

east toward Fifth. They'll send a squad car after you."

She hung up. Anna stood looking at her, waiting. "He's calling your mother," Isabel told her.

Anna nodded gravely. "Ben," she called, her voice worn down to a hoarse croak.

They made their way east as best they could. The paths meandered here. It was the slowest part of Manhattan, no sharp-angled intersections and street signs, only curving paths. Finally, Isabel saw the gray tops of the buildings along Fifth Avenue. The traffic noise grew louder. She and Anna had to scream more forcefully to make any impact against it.

"Your phone is going off," Anna told her.

Isabel answered it.

Luke said, "I'm in the car. Is Anna okay?"

"Yeah, she's fine. She's helping me look."

"Did you reach Jackie?" Isabel asked him.

"She's on the way."

"How is she taking it?"

His voice had an edge that cut her. "How do you think she's taking it?" Then, he said, "I'm sorry."

"No, of course."

He said, "When you get to Fifth, call me. The cops are waiting to hear." He hung up.

She thought of the *New York Post*. It was the weirdest thing to think of, but her insides were shrieking like a *Post* headline, and this was the stuff of which those headlines were made. Ben dismembered in some dank corner of the park. Ben in a Dumpster. Ben in the East River. She wanted to go back, just go back to the time of the shoot, and lose the light. Forget the light. Light could be faked. You could burn the spots, get what you needed. You could fake it. But Ben . . .

Anna was quiet. She wasn't even calling anymore. She clung to Isabel's hand. What was she thinking?

Isabel stopped and pulled Anna against her. She squeezed her hard. "I'm sorry, Anna," she said. "I'm sorry."

Anna squeezed her back.

They broke loose and turned the corner onto Fifth. She lifted the phone, got ready to dial. It began to throb. Her cell phone rang. She clutched at it. Her fingers were shaking so hard, she could hardly flip it open.

It was Luke. "They found him, Isabel," he said. "He's okay. He's just fine."

"Oh, God," she said, collapsing onto the nearest bench.

"Where is he?"

"He's here. At the station house. I'm looking at him right now."

Isabel began to cry. She couldn't even say goodbye. Anna took the phone from her, spoke to her father, and Isabel put her head down on her knees and wept with relief.

Anna stood there, watching wordlessly as Isabel wept into her hands and thought that she would never be able to lift her face out of her shame and her misery. She would never be able to look at Anna, lurking there at her elbow, judging. She would never be able to face Luke, her poor Luke. She loved him so much and had failed him so hugely. And Jackie, how could she ever meet Jackie's eye again?

Anna said, "There's the police car."

Isabel cried all the way to the station house. She cried harder when she saw Luke standing at the desk, doing paperwork. He caught her eye and nodded toward a bench by the wall. She sat there with Anna and watched Ben, legs dangling on the police sergeant's desk, doing his act for several policemen. The boy was grinning, thrilled to have an audience of grown-ups, especially grown-ups in uniforms. For Isabel, the whole world had collapsed inside her at the thought of harm coming to him, and there he sat now as though nothing had changed, nothing had happened.

Jackie blew in the door and ran down the corridor toward them, past them: to Ben. She grabbed him to her, like a rag doll. She was holding him. She was shaking furiously. "Ben, oh my Ben. Are you all right?" She held him only far enough away to examine him.

"I knew where I was all the time," he told her.

The desk sergeant said, "We found him in the zoo."

Jackie's eyes, her burning eyes, found Isabel. They scorched her.

Then, she turned to Anna and said fiercely, "Stay here with your brother. Hold his hand. Don't let go of him."

Isabel was trembling. It had moved out from her heart and into every limb, every finger. She stood to face Jackie with her apology, lame as it was. It was all she had now. "Jackie," she said. "I am so sorry. I just looked away for one second. I never even . . ."

Jackie ignored her and turned instead to Luke. "Listen carefully," she said in an even, terrible voice. "I'm only going to say this once. That woman has nothing more to do with my children."

"Our children," Luke said.

"Do you realize what could have happened to your son? How lucky we are the police found him before some lunatic did? He could have been . . ." She couldn't finish.

Isabel didn't blame her. She couldn't finish that thought either.

"Jackie," Luke said soothingly. "Let's not make this any worse. Isabel's sorry. But it could have happened to anyone . . ."

"Not to me," she said with hot conviction.

"Jackie, you've made some mistakes," he said. "We all make mistakes . . ."

"I'm not going to wait around to see the next one," she said, leaning into his face. "I'm not going to watch my children fall through the cracks of this arrangement. I'm seeing a lawyer."

Luke stiffened. "Jackie, stop. We promised we'd never go there."

Jackie leveled him with a look. She said, "We've broken a lot of promises, haven't we, Luke?"

Isabel's pain turned in one instant to anger, a chemical reaction. She couldn't let this happen to Luke. It wasn't his fault. He would never have lost Ben. It was her fault, squarely hers, only hers. She stepped closer to Jackie, made herself meet and hold Jackie's eyes. "Why are you taking this out on him?"

"Isabel, please," Luke said, trying to stop this from happening. "It's best if you st—"

But Isabel wouldn't stay out of it, couldn't stay out of it. She was in it up to the part in her hair.

She had caused it. She said, "You haven't done one goddamn thing to make any of this easier."

"I am not here to make it easier for you," Jackie said. "These are my children. They don't want to be with you."

"Maybe they would," Isabel said.

"What?" Jackie's eyes flashed.

"If they thought it met with your approval," Isabel said.

Jackie pivoted away from Isabel and latched on to Luke with her ferocity. "A court order is going to say that woman is never alone with my children. Ever again."

She grabbed each of her children by a hand and stormed out of the station. And as much as Isabel ached for how Jackie had turned it on Luke, she couldn't really blame the other woman for her feelings, for blaming her so much. Isabel blamed herself that much. Probably more.

JACKIE

She took the children riding. It was as much for herself as for them. Since childhood, Jackie had always turned to horses for solace. Being in the saddle put her above the meanest things in life, let her see over the top of them. And kept her moving away from whatever it was that troubled her. However she felt when she mounted, she felt lighter when she landed back on the ground, when she came back to standing on her own two feet. She could go on. Because, anyway, she had to go on.

The day was brilliant. The first leaves were turning yellow and red on the trees, yet the hillsides were still a lush green. She breathed deeply.

Ben did not seem any worse for wear, given what he had been through. But then, what had he been through really? He got to strike out on his own through the forest of Manhattan, in search of wild beasts. And he had found them—sea lions and monkeys and a pacing lion. He had gotten to hold a policeman's baton, and ride in the squad car with the lights flashing. They had let him turn on the siren. What more could a boy wish for?

Still, he was quiet now. After a while on the trail,

he said, "Mommy, it's not Isabel's fault I ran away."

Jackie agreed. "No. That's your fault. It's *her* fault for not watching over my precious son, as if it were her priority. Which means, her most important job."

Ben considered this. "Isabel's job is she works."

"Ben," Jackie said, "mommies work, too. They work very hard. I work harder as a mom than I did when I was working. I just don't get paid."

Anna asked, "Does Isabel make a lot of money?"

"People like Isabel who only think about themselves often make a lot of money."

Both children mulled this over, and then Ben said, "I think she's pretty."

Jackie grinned at him wryly. "Yes, if you like big teeth."

They all laughed.

"Mommy?" Ben asked after a little more thought.

"What, honey?"

"If you want me to hate her, I will."

Which paralyzed Jackie. A feeling spread through her, like venom. It spread along her arms and through her chest and went deep inside. It was very much like shame.

LUKE

He couldn't sit still that night, and Isabel wasn't speaking much. She couldn't even bring herself to look at him. So Luke paced from one end of the loft to the other, listening to the awful rhythm of Isabel's exercise machine. She was relentless.

What had happened with Ben had been awful for him. His heart had stopped when Isabel called. He had gone instantly numb. And if it hadn't been for the saving necessity of the phone calls he had to make, he would have been paralyzed by the very idea of what might be happening to his little son. But there had been the phone calls to make; there had been purpose. He had had to get himself down to the police station, and by then, they had found Ben and were on their way in with him.

It was a short acquaintance with terror. But not short enough. He had asked himself how Isabel could have let it happen. He would have asked her. But, driving home, it was clear she was questioning herself. And all her answers were harsh. With her head held straight up, her eyes fixed ahead of her, she had sat next to him and cried silently all the way downtown.

Later, when he had put together something to

eat—they had to eat—he had pushed her to talk to him. She insisted that she agreed with Jackie: She didn't deserve the responsibility of his children. She had proven that, she said. Maybe she didn't deserve him either. She had said that more than once. Maybe she should just leave, then Jackie would have no reason to bring a lawyer into the mix.

Luke had never seen her like this. Isabel was the most confident person he had ever known. Anybody acquainted with both the women in his life—Jackie and Isabel—would have scoffed at that assessment. Jackie Harrison exuded self-assurance. She had an aura of knowing exactly what she wanted and knowing precisely how to get it. But the truth was— and you couldn't live with someone for decades without discovering her secrets—the truth was that Jackie questioned herself. She would take a stand right up front and defend it to the bitterest end. But she had her doubts working away at her underneath. She had trouble sleeping. Always had.

Isabel slept like a child. She lived in the world like a child, as if it belonged to her. Here she was working in a field populated by incredibly neurotic egos, and she just laughed them off, navigated through them. She didn't take Duncan seriously. She didn't take the ad execs seriously. She didn't take herself seriously. It was simply that she always knew what was the right next move—or so it seemed to him. It was inborn, her confidence. It was instinctive. She possessed herself completely.

And now she was shaken. Completely. Kids could do that to you. He had tried to tell her about the first time his infant daughter had wailed for twelve hours straight—that rocked your sense of self, your understanding of your own power. Suddenly you were helpless to help a creature who was helpless even to explain herself. You couldn't stop the pain. You couldn't stop the noise. You couldn't soothe her to sleep. You couldn't sleep yourself. So much for high honors in law school. So much for million-dollar settlements. You could do *nothing*.

Isabel didn't seem to hear him. She listened. But it didn't seem to soak in. One thing about being in charge of herself so wholly was that she was the only one whose judgment meant anything. She was the only one who could let herself off the hook—or keep herself strung up. There was no comforting Isabel. She had to work some of it out on her own.

He went and stood by her now and waited for her to acknowledge him. She didn't. Her face was stony and wet. She had stopped crying. She was just sweating it out, flight fifty-six and counting. He only hoped that she would climb all the way out of it—and find her way back to him.

"I'm going for a drive," he told her.

"Be safe," she said. That's all.

Luke stood and looked at her a minute longer. She stared out at the city lights and kept climbing the invisible staircase to nowhere. There was nothing he could do for her, he realized. Isabel took care of Isabel. But maybe he could help himself. Maybe he could help the children. He could appeal to Jackie.

He used Anna's soccer clothes as an excuse for driving to Nyack. The traffic was sparser at this hour on a weeknight, and it felt good to give the car a stab of gas—and just go. Luke could drive these roads without thinking about it.

The kids' bedroom lights were already off when he arrived. Only the downstairs was still lighted, and something in him tightened at the sight of it: home. How many times had he turned this corner, coming from the train? How many times had he looked up to see the windows full of light and known that they were waiting?

No one was waiting now. Jackie was out on the front porch, though, watering her plants in the dark. "What do you want?" she asked. Not nicely.

He didn't go up on the porch. He felt a barrier that had not been there before today, not between her and him. It was palpable now. If he reached out his hand, he might touch it. So he stayed where he was, only held up the bundle of soccer clothes. "Anna left her stuff at my house. Figured she'd need it this week . . ."

Jackie nodded and continued watering her plants.

He worked up the words. "Did you see the lawyer?"

"Called him," she said tersely. "I have an appointment. Day after tomorrow."

"Don't do this," he said softly. He felt the way he used to feel when they were married and an argument would drag into the night, into bed with them. He felt the way he had when he would have done anything to make her happy enough to let him rest, happy enough that she could sleep herself.

Jackie sighed, looking at him the way she would look at him then—when they both had endured as much as they could stand, when all she could do was touch his hand in the night and release him until morning. She said, "You're saying don't put the kids through a war. But I'm doing this for their well-being."

"Partly," he said. "But partly, you're mad."

She looked at him.

"You know the kids aren't really in danger."

She didn't argue. She gave him the opening, at least.

He said, "This is about Isabel. I know she made a mistake. But she's trying . . . she's learning."

She bristled with skepticism. "Slugs have faster learning curves. Trees even. Clams."

"Give her some time. Please. Don't drive her away."

"I'm supposed to care about her?" There was bitterness in her voice.

"You're supposed to care about me," he said gently. "Like I care about you."

She looked at him hard. "Like you cared about me three years ago when you walked out that door?"

"You kicked me out."

And here it goes again, he thought, as they worked themselves back into the loop of the never-ending battle. He held up a palm. "Look," he told her. "Let's not go there, okay?"

She kept watering.

"Don't do this thing with the lawyers. The kids will be okay." He paused. "If we're okay."

She looked at him.

"Help me here," he asked her. "I'd do it for you."

She closed her eyes slowly, then opened them. She looked away, her eyes sweeping out across the river that was invisible in the darkness but was there all the same, always, was there like whatever still ran between them, however invisible it had become, however submerged. The river was still there, running toward the sea, as surely as some current still coursed between Jackie and himself—no matter what barriers had gone up, no matter the years apart and all the angry words. No matter Isabel.

"One last chance," Jackie said, then turned and opened the screen door to go inside. "Don't make me regret it."

ISABEL

Isabel had printed up every picture from the Rapunzel shoot. Luke had taken a dawn flight to Pittsburgh (again), and she had gotten to the studio early, fueled by Starbucks. She had disappeared into the darkroom. It was her favorite place to be, actually, full of the sound of water and stillness. Cooper teased her that it was like returning to the womb for her. And he didn't know how close he came to the truth: Working there was her greatest comfort. Only there could she capture light on paper, only there could she save something that was otherwise so fleeting.

As a kid, she had played hard, and now that she was grown and her photography was just a form of play for which she got paid, she worked hard. Grandma Celie had said that their Issy had gone full throttle from dawn to dusk so the demons couldn't get a toehold in her. That was Grandma, a good Baptist. But Isabel could see the truth in it sometimes. If you didn't settle, you couldn't think about your troubles. You drove the demons out. Even tenacious demons like Jackie Harrison.

When she emerged, late in the afternoon, Duncan was pleased with the shots, and it was winding down into a discussion of which pose most revealed the musculature of Prince Charming, or whichever prince this was supposed to be anyway. Everyone was gathered around the studio's worktable, discussing and shuffling and reshuffling and discussing again—showing off their opinions like kids showing off their biceps.

The phone rang. Cooper answered, then handed it over to Isabel. "Anna's school," he said. "They're looking for Luke."

Isabel squeezed her eyebrows together. Why? Then she took the phone. "He's in Pittsburgh," she told the school secretary on the other end. And then she listened in amazement: Jackie hadn't shown up to pick up the kids after school. Isabel said, "That's impossible. You must have the wrong kids."

But, no, the woman said, this was Anna and Ben Harrison. No doubt.

"No way," Isabel said. "Jackie Harrison never forgets, is never late, is never imperfect. She would never forget to pick up her kids . . ." Isabel knew she was going way overboard, but, hey: It felt good. She wasn't the only screwup. "You're absolutely sure it's them?"

Duncan hissed, "Isabel, may I remind you that the clients are arriving at four-thi—"

"Sure. No problem," Isabel told the secretary. "I'll pick them up."

Duncan shot her a withering look.

"Don't worry," she told him. "I'll be back. On time."

He was furious, and after she left, she could just imagine what he would say to Cooper and the others. Probably, "She's dangling on my last nerve." That was one of his favorite pearls. As she left the room, she could feel his glare on her back, hot as a spotlight.

But how many opportunities like this one did she get. To be there when Jackie had fouled up. Royally.

Only when she got to Nyack and saw the kids waiting for their mother, it wasn't so sweet anymore. It was strangely sad. They were sitting side by side, glum. And confused.

Anna looked up. Isabel could see Anna's expectation of seeing her mother change into disappointment at seeing Isabel instead. Something in Isabel reached for the girl then and didn't blame her at all for her reaction. Something in Isabel understood that disappointment. She held out a bag of potato chips she had poached from the studio kitchen. "Barbecue," she said. "I know they're your favorite."

No takers. The kids were intently staring at their shoes again. Isabel sat down beside them.

Anna said, "How could she just . . . forget us?"

"Yeah," Ben agreed. He shrugged at Isabel. "That's something *you* would do."

Isabel ate a chip and decided to lie. "Tell ya the truth," she said confidentially, "I did."

Anna and Ben blinked. What?

"Your mom had to . . . help a friend with this . . . emergency. And she called me. And we switched days. Then I got stuck on my shoot. Forgot all about you."

The kids nodded. It made perfect sense. This, they could accept. This squared with the logic of their world.

And then Anna looked past Isabel and cried,

"Mommy!" Both children skirted Isabel and fell upon their mother, who gathered them in and swept them back down the hall. Her eyes barely acknowledged Isabel's presence. In a minute they were gone, and Isabel was left on a hard wooden bench, eating barbecue potato chips in a deserted school and knowing she was going to be late for the meeting with the clients. There was no way she could make it.

That would have been that. Isabel would have made her apologies to Duncan by wowing the clients: Better late than never. (Also, she had brought him a lime tart from Dean & DeLuca's the next morning.) Life would have gone on. Luke's ex be damned.

Except the next day Jackie showed up at the studio while Isabel was working in the darkroom. Isabel was just hanging a photo to dry, and she switched on the lights so her eyes could adjust even as her mind tried to: What was *she* doing here?

Jackie said, "Look, I'm not real comfortable being here."

"I don't recall inviting you."

A long pause. Jackie looked at her, looked away. Finally she said, "I overheard what you told Anna and Ben yesterday."

"I hate a snoop."

"I didn't need you to take the blame for me," Jackie said.

"I didn't do it for you. Believe me." Isabel shrugged. "They already hate me. You've seen to that."

Jackie said, "You're not terribly good at taking

care of them. Kids sense inexperience and uncertainty."

"I just need practice."

"Those are my children you're practicing on. Make some of your own kids and practice on them."

Isabel sighed. Now Jackie was going to start tracking her down to the refuge of her own workplace—to harangue her. How was she supposed to go on like this?

Jackie seemed genuinely curious, tenaciously curious. "So why did you . . . ?"

"I did it for them." Isabel looked straight in Jackie's eyes when she said it. "Poor kids have to believe in something. Even if it is you." She knew she didn't sound one bit friendly. But she didn't feel one bit friendly toward this woman. Isabel was in the middle of this because of Luke. Not because of Jackie. Not even because of the kids. Sure the kids were adorable (when they were asleep), and occasionally they were so totally like Luke that she thought she loved them, like when Ben smelled his socks after taking them off or when Anna sang show tunes in the shower. But Isabel was up to her clavicle in this mess because, one, she loved Luke Harrison, and two, she had a soft heart and sometimes the kids got to it. Sometimes she knew what they were feeling, how out of control of their grown-ups they felt. And even if they had no inkling of her empathy and didn't care to know, still, she did understand something of what they were going through. And if it would make them feel better for her to cast their mother in a good light, then so what? That was about Anna and Ben. It wasn't about Jackie. Isabel smirked. She turned the screw, couldn't resist turning it tighter into this smug woman. She said, "It's strange. Impossible really."

"What?"

"That you forgot them." She latched on to Jackie's eyes. "Where the hell were you?"

Jackie shifted her eyes. She changed the subject. "Look," she said. "I have another appointment this afternoon. And since Luke is away, I need someone else to take them to the park."

Isabel scoffed. "And have federal agents jump out of the bushes with court ordrs? How many years do you get in this state for giving second-rate care to minors?"

"However many, it's not enough."

"I'm already on thin ice. Yesterday, when I ran out of here . . . I actually thought my boss was going to fire me."

"Fine. Forget it." Jackie turned to go.

Isabel's first thought was that if Jackie weren't such a controlling witch and if she would just have normal friendships, she wouldn't have to ask her sworn enemy for this favor. But Jackie was a controlling witch. And she didn't have anyone else to turn to. But that didn't mean Isabel had to wreck her day and put herself in more jeopardy with Duncan . . .

Then she thought of the kids, of how forlorn they had looked yesterday, how expendable. And she thought of how much confidence Luke was entrusting in her, despite her huge mistakes. She sighed. "Wait. I'll do it. I can swing it."

Jackied nodded, obviously relieved. She emptied her purse on the counter, narrating instructively:

"Kleenex. Band-Aids for cuts. Neosporin for infection. Tylenol for fever . . ."

"Why not just bring the whole pharmacy?" Isabel quipped.

Jackie didn't alter her purpose. "Ben likes to be read to," she said. "Do you know Dr. Seuss?"

"Not personally."

"Do you have a word limit you need to hit every day, or can I finish?"

Isabel shut up.

Jackie handed her a Post-it. "Here's their schedule for this afternoon."

Isabel took it, then thought she might as well float the idea she'd woken up thinking about two days ago. "Okay, now that you're here I wanted to ask you . . . See, the place where I might be able to connect with Anna is music. And there's this Pearl Jam concert next Thursday . . ."

Jackie shut her down with a look. Then she said, "You want to take an eleven-year-old girl to a Pearl Jam concert? On a school night?"

Isabel shrugged. "Well, yeah. Just the two of us."

"Forget it. She's too young."

Isabel tried to keep her anger from getting loose. Or was it hurt? Didn't one good turn deserve another? In Grandma Celie's world, it had. "Okay," she said. "Fine."

Jackie turned to go. "I'll meet you at the park at five. All I ask is that my children are alive when I get there."

As the door closed behind her lover's ex-wife, Isabel's spurned curiosity explored all the possibilities for why Jackie—who clearly despised her—

would come right into her territory. It had to have cost Jackie a lot to ask a favor of Isabel, especially this particular favor. Jackie would only have done it for something that meant a lot to her, and what could that be? What could that be . . . but love? *Jackie's having an affair*, Isabel told herself smugly. *Jackie Harrison is having an affair. Nothing but love would make her turn her kids over to me.*

JACKIE

It was the stillness that got to her. It was having to lie motionless while she was moved through the machine, nothing but matter on a conveyor belt. Keeping her body still seemed to provoke her mind to prove that it was something else altogether, something untethered to any weakness of mere cells. It could go where it wanted. The machine would never know, could never see into its journeys. And so her mind flitted into dark corners of worry but didn't linger anywhere long before ricocheting off to the next: the possibility of Isabel letting Ben fall off the seesaw. The origin of Anna's headache that morning. And the chance her own cancer had come back, that lump in her breast that she'd told no one about.

Then her mind would swing back to brighter possibilities. Last year when she'd had the lump removed and had radiation therapy, the doctors had assured her they had it all. There was next to no possibility that it would recur. So she thought this for reassurance, and then she swung back to the chance that the cancer had come back, and that she might have to say good-bye to her children and mean forever. She returned to what the doctors had said last time, and then back again to the chance that the cancer had come back anyway, that it was lurking, waiting. Despite what the doctors thought. That was the one worry her mind kept darting over to and then running away from: Maybe it had come back.

Maybe it hadn't.

This machine would know what her chances were. It probably already knew. It was whispering and lisping to itself, looking deep inside her, through her skin and into her bones and her organs. It lisped to her blood, told it what secrets it knew. And her blood ran cold inside her, all through her.

Jackie thought she would never stop shaking, even after she was out of the flimsy gown and dressed in her own thickly woven and familiar clothes again. She thought she would never warm up. But when she was sitting in the doctor's office, when she had seen the doctor's face—in that first glance—she had grown hot. It was as though she had swallowed acid. She burned.

Dr. Sweikert was a kind doctor. But she was like a good friend who couldn't keep the truth out of her eyes. And sometimes the truth was not kind.

"It's spread?"

The doctor nodded.

"But I've been doing everything right." Even as she said it, Jackie knew it was a useless appeal. And stupid.

"We found some spots through the MRI," Dr. Sweikert said. "And the biopsy of your lymph nodes came back positive. It's in three of them."

"But last time . . ." Sometimes she couldn't switch off the part of herself that demanded logic from medicine and marriage and life. "You said you got it all. So you could be wrong again. Last time you said one thing, and now . . ."

"Last time was a year ago." The doctor paused. This was hard for her too, no matter how many times she had to do it. Jackie could see that. Dr. Sweikert said, "That was a tiny lump. We treated it with radiation. We thought we had it all. We were hopeful. But there were no guarantees."

Jackie tried to breathe. She wanted to maintain control, her composure. She wanted to be brave. She had always admired bravery in the seriously ill, admired a nobility of spirit that could lift someone above the terror of her circumstance. But her truest impulse was to cry: She wanted to live. "But we can beat it?" She looked across the desk to the doctor, met her eye, asked for hope. "People beat it. Don't they? All the time."

Dr. Sweikert didn't miss a beat. She nodded. "Every day. More and more."

Jackie swallowed back sudden tears. Permission to hope had weakened her. She could hope. She could. "So what's next? Another round of radiation?"

Dr. Sweikert shook her head. "Chemo."

Jackie felt it like a blow. She absorbed it. This kind of hope had borders. "That's necessary, huh?"

"Let's take our best shot."

Jackie nodded, looked at her watch. Why did she need the hour as an excuse though? She wanted to get out of here. That was as good a reason as any, just wanting to. Needing to. "You'll excuse me," she told the doctor. "I have to pick up the kids."

The doctor leaned toward her, detained Jackie

with her voice, its gravity. "You should tell your husband this time."

Jackie shook her head. "Why would his worry, or my children's worry, or anyone's worry . . . help the situation?"

"Sooner than later," the doctor said, softly, gently. "You really need to. Maybe ask him to dinner."

"You don't burden others needlessly. That's how I was raised, Doctor."

Dr. Sweikert nodded. She did understand. But her eyes said, *Now understand me.* When she spoke, it was to reiterate her position. "Ask him to dinner."

LUKE

This was the part that made him nervous. Facing Jackie. Sometimes it felt as though she wasn't only the mother of his children, but his mother as well. That's what you got from spending years of your life with someone, the years when you were learning who you were, who you would be. You took cues from the person there with you, judged yourself by how she judged you. In the end, that had been the problem, hadn't it?

So why hang on to that pattern now? Why let her matter so much? He couldn't answer himself that one. Saying it was for the kids wasn't saying it all.

Luke figured it was just as well that she had called him to set up dinner. Otherwise, he would have had to call her to arrange a meeting, or he would have gone up to the house on some flimsy errand, and she would have been on edge, suspicious of his motives: What was up? This way, he could camouflage his news with whatever it was she was here to discuss—how Isabel left her diaphragm on the bathroom sink where Anna had found it or how Isabel let the kids eat candy made with red dye, or how Isabel had slipped up and said the F-word within earshot of Ben, the parrot. (Only the way

Jackie put it, you'd think Isabel had sat the kid down and drilled the word into him when actually she had stubbed her toe on a metal plant stand, and Ben just happened to be across the loft and down the hall with his ears turned on high.)

He and Jackie were meeting at a French place where they had gone together often during their marriage. Her choice. There was a fireplace and a publike bar, and years ago when they had been living in their cramped West Side apartment, Jackie had said it felt like going home, eating at this particular restaurant. It was what a real home should be. Not two rooms, a galley kitchen, and a bathroom with no windows. This restaurant was part of her persuasion in moving them, years later, to Nyack. Priming him for what she wanted.

Jackie was waiting. She had a drink, and she looked up from it in greeting. "You look pretty," he told her, bending to kiss her cheek. And she did. She was wearing burgundy, a rich color made richer by the auburn of her hair, and by the flush of her cheeks. She did look pretty, younger than she had in a while.

But mostly it was his mood speaking, the exhilaration of beginning something that he had dreaded, beginning to get it over with. He took a sip of Jackie's cocktail, and indicated to the waitress that he would take the same. Already, he was getting that surge of energy that urged him on at the beginning of a contest, when he knew he had to get in there and scrabble for what he wanted, or needed. "I'm glad you called because I have something to tell you, too," he said.

She looked surprised. But she smiled. "Well?"

"You first," he said.

"No, you."

"No, go ahead."

They laughed. He laid his hands on the table, and said, "I'm going to ask Isabel to marry me."

Jackie tried to keep her face the same, but her features twitched, trying to move in the direction of whatever it was she felt. He couldn't tell.

He said, "I know you don't think much of her. But she's a special person. She really is."

"Why are you telling me this?" Her tone was not unkind. It was slightly incredulous.

"I want you to tell me that it's okay."

She sat up straighter, prouder. "You don't need my approval."

"The kids do."

The waitress brought his drink and asked if they needed anything else, and Luke had grown so tense that he answered, "Yeah, a little less service." She retreated.

Luke sighed. He wanted this to go well. He needed it to. Isabel was the very heart of his happiness. She had granted him the gift of acceptance; she loved him for who he was: oldish and baldish and all. And he could not risk losing her. He had come too close, and now he had to prove to her that he trusted her completely—with his children, with himself, with the rest of his life. He needed Isabel, and he needed to secure her place next to him and his next to her.

Which, of course, he could not say to Jackie. Still, he had to have her help. Anna and Ben took their cues from their mother, and if Jackie knew that he was serious about Isabel, maybe she would settle

into the notion of it. Maybe she could adjust to it—
and help the kids adjust. "Look," he said. "It's
going to be hard for the kids. And . . . I think we
should tell them together."

"To make it easier for them?" she asked. "Or
you?" A sharpness was creeping in.

He just looked at her.

She said, "You can't be an 'us' just when you
want to. You can't play that card when it's convenient."

"We . . ."

"*We* are over." Her voice was hard. It had a
knife's edge.

He countered, "We're still their parents for the
next hundred years."

She looked down and then away, over his shoulder into the fire. Her face changed. When she spoke
again, her voice was soft, the old Jackie's, the one
he hadn't heard in a long long while. It was solemn,
maybe even sad. It had no fight in it. "What makes
you think this marriage will work any better than
ours?"

Though she brought her eyes to his, he couldn't
hold them. He looked away.

She sighed then.

And it was as if that sigh stole the breath from
his own lungs. He couldn't answer her that one.

They sat for a long moment, looking into their
drinks. He hadn't meant to make her miserable.
That was the last thing he would have expected. He
had only wanted her help. She was always so busy
being a fortress that he forgot it was all in the effort
to protect what was most tender in her, what was
most vulnerable. He had forgotten—conveniently

allowed himself to forget—that there was a part of Jackie that could still be hurt by him. There was a part of her that still cared, no matter how little she showed it. He hated the look in her eyes, that sadness. He hated being the cause of it. "How about your news?" he asked finally, trying to steer them back to ground that didn't shift under them.

She smiled weakly, met his eyes, and shook her head slowly. "Let's glory in yours," she said wryly.

ISABEL

Isabel woke with Luke kissing her. It was like waking into a good dream. The light coming through the loft windows was early light, too early for a Saturday morning, for her. But Luke had been up for a while already, padding around in his boxers and tee. She could smell the coffee from the kitchen. He had come back to bed to give her a kiss. She smiled.

"Wake up," he murmured against her eyelids, when she had closed them again, not sure she wanted to surface all the way into the day. Not yet. It was nice here in the early light with Luke brushing his lips against her temple. Nice. "Wake up."

Isabel pulled herself up on the pillows. He was in soft focus, and she tried to think how to replicate that effect—a sleep filter—with her photography. She tried to think . . .

Luke was smiling at her, watchfully.

She smiled back.

He handed her a small black box. She tried to understand what it could mean, thought she did. She opened it. But inside there was only a spool of brown thread. She quizzed him with a look.

He said, "It seems to me if two people are going to spend their lives together, there has to be a certain tenacity . . ." He was tying the thread to her finger, so gently, and then he unraveled the thread, pulled it back toward himself.

Her gaze shifted from the knotted thread to his eyes, to that look in his eyes, which she loved.

"You have to hold on to each other," he told her. "Even if it's just by a thread at times."

Oh, Luke, she thought. *Oh, Luke. Yes, yes, yes.*

"I let that thread break once," he said with gravity. "This time, I won't."

He lifted his end of the thread, and a diamond engagement ring slid down it, so gently, a slow fall. It slid down the thread and onto Isabel's finger.

It was beautiful, sparkling there. But she couldn't take her eyes off Luke, not for long. She couldn't take herself away from that look in his eyes, that look that said he knew what she wanted and he wanted it, too, at whatever cost and through whatever effort and despite any mistakes she might make or he might make—and he wanted it forever.

"I won't let it break either," she told him, so that he smiled and drew her to him in a long embrace that ended with a kiss. Sealed. A vow.

JACKIE

It was the kind of day when change itself seemed to carry on the wind, the kind of day that made her ache with nostalgia for the moment she was living Right Now. Walking across the lawn, Jackie passed through layers of summer air still stirring, warm currents. But mainly the colder, crisper air was pushing in as if it was carried down the Hudson, dispatched from the north.

The trees seemed to give off light through their yellow and orange and red leaves. Raking the leaves that had already fallen, she paused and lifted her eyes to the sky. She looked at the burnished leaves, bold as brass against the blue. She filled herself with the way it looked. She wanted to remember. She wanted to take that light inside her and have it burn always.

She wanted to believe in always. And on a day like today, it seemed possible: Things were always changing. Wasn't that the only permanence?

This morning Anna and Ben had crawled into bed with her, and they had talked about the Halloween costumes Jackie was making them. She was like the designer of their dreams when it came to wardrobe concerns. Each year, in the month approaching

Halloween, they told her about an idea that had come to them when they were trying to fall asleep, and she told them if it was doable or not. For them, she made most things doable. This morning the question had been whether Anna's real hair could be disguised under a man's duck-tailed puff. Jackie's opinion was that it could.

Today, they had talked until hunger had driven them out from under the covers. Then, Ben had squealed at the brisk air, and they had all walked on their toes going into the tile bathroom: cold on bare feet. "The frost is on the pumpkin," Anna cried, a signal. And Ben had said, "It's time. It's time." And they had gone downstairs to make the first pumpkin muffins of the year: Anna mixed the dry ingredients, Jackie the wet, and Ben spooned the batter into the muffin cups (and pinched a spare chocolate chip or two). Pumpkin muffins were a family tradition on the first truly chilly weekend of fall.

It's what made a life, Jackie thought, the rituals anchored in the flow of time. People measured their lives not so much by hours or months, but rather by the rituals they anticipated and then recalled: the things that stayed the same no matter how things evolved around them. Life was made of dreaming up homemade Halloween costumes and baking pumpkin muffins and planting tulip bulbs in the circle bed. It was made of eating s'mores on the first night the fireplace got lighted and stringing popcorn streamers for the Christmas tree. Daddies might come and go, even mommies, but the seasons would still bring their own expectations. There would still be moments anchored in familiar acts.

In the afternoon, Jackie and the children raked leaves together for a while, and then Ben insisted that Anna push him in the tree swing. His laughter came out of him like party streamers, trailing in the arc of his motion. Jackie closed her eyes, memorized the sound of it.

It was crazy, raking this early in the autumn. There were days and days of raining leaves to come. But, still, Jackie raked, just to be here in the sunshine with her children, to be in the sunshine. The doctor would do everything in her power, and Jackie would match the efforts. But her most pressing job now was to eke meaning out of every moment. Every moment.

Of course it was Ben who saw the possibility in the work she had done, in that great mountain of leaves. He plunged right in.

"You're ruining it," Anna scolded. "Isn't he, Mom?"

"Yes," Jackie said. And she plunged in, too, buried herself.

Anna landed on her, giggling.

And that was how Luke found them. It might have been any day, Luke coming home from the hardware store or the tire shop. It might have just been Luke coming home from weekend work in the city. But both children sat up in surprise when they spotted him: He didn't belong here anymore.

Jackie saw how surprised they were. She should have told them that he was coming. But the day had its own momentum, and now here he was, as if by some of Ben's better magic.

Luke grinned at the kids. And they looked at

Jackie. She grinned back at them: Everything's okay.

Still, Anna was suspicious when they all trooped up onto the porch and settled into the wicker furniture. "Why are you guys acting so weird?"

"What do you mean?" Jackie said, still picking the leaves out of her hair."

"You're both smiling way too much."

Jackie guessed they were maybe. A week ago, she was not sure she could have mustered any gaiety for this particular family meeting. But today, it seemed easy. Today it seemed the easiest of all the things she had to face, that they would have to face. This was a simple lesson in living. In coping. This was an easy thing to tell her children. Compared to what else there was to tell.

It was odd, not only that Luke was suddenly blended back into the context of their lives at home, but also that they were all of them wrapped in their cold-weather jackets and hanging out on the porch. The porch was for summertime. They might have gone inside where it was warm, where there was a fire. But the fresh air was too good, and Jackie couldn't give it up.

Jackie tried to open things up. "The great thing about life is that things keep changing," she said.

And Luke added, "Remember when Mommy and Daddy got divorced?"

"And we all went through that together," Jackie said.

Both children sat warily, as if bullets were about to be fired into their soft flesh. Jackie couldn't bear the look of them, her poor little ones. Subject to the whims of their grown-ups. Subject to the whims of life itself.

"Well," Luke told them. "Things are going to change again."

"I knew it," Ben said. "I knew you guys would get back together."

Jackie looked at Luke, and Anna saw the look. She understood immediately. "No, they're not," she said.

"What?" Ben asked, as if only he had been left out of the secret plan.

"Daddy's gonna marry Isabel." Anna said it like an announcement, a spiteful, joyless announcement.

Ben's face shifted into hurt. He turned a questioning look to his father, who nodded.

Anna turned red. It started in her nose, the way it always did. Jackie reached for her daughter. "Don't get upset . . ."

"I'm not upset," Anna said with fury. "Why should I even care? I mean, nobody asked me when you got divorced. Nobody asked me if I wanted a new mother. Nobody even asked me if I like her. If you guys don't care about our family staying together, why should I?"

"Daddy and I tried hard," Jackie told her. "We really did."

Ben blurted out: "No, you didn't. All you guys did was name-call. I heard you. You didn't even try and use your words." His dark little head was pivoting. He looked from his mother to his father. "What am I supposed to call her now anyway?"

Jackie looked at Luke, and Luke put his arm around their son, comforting him. "Guys," Jackie told the children, "Isabel's not taking my place as

your mother . . ." And inside, she prayed that this
was true, would always be true.

"No," Luke backed her up. "This is just . . .
It's something that's important to me. This doesn't
change the way I feel about you."

Neither of the children looked ready to buy any
of this.

Jackie leaned onto her knees, looked from one
to the other as she told them: "Life is full of hard
things. It's not always fair. But we do have a choice
to make things better. Instead of worse."

"Like how?" Anna pressed.

"Like seeing the good side of Isabel. And what
she brings to your father's life. And your life."

Saying that even got Luke's attention. And Anna
was boring her eyes into her mother's. This is not
what she had expected. Not from Jackie. But this
was the lesson, the first lesson and easiest. It was
important. Jackie went on, "Because the time comes
in every family when you need to be there. For each
other."

She reached over and stroked Anna's hair.

Anna was gazing at her so calmly: As if she suddenly understood. "I'll be there for you," she told
her mother, so sincerely, so sponteously, so much
like the little girl who had once looked up from her
bath and said, "I'll never love anyone, Mommy, the
way I love you." That same little baby girl.

Jackie pulled her daughter close and breathed in
the salty sweetness of Anna's quirky hair part and
whispered what was in her heart: "I'm counting on
it."

ISABEL

Luke was tied up over courtroom trouble and wasn't home yet. Ben had fallen asleep halfway through *The Stinky Cheese Man*—which Isabel could now recite from memory—and Anna was working on an art project. With Ben zonked and the puppy wound down into a slumberous hump, the loft was finally quiet enough for Isabel to get some of her work done.

In the old days, pre-Luke, she would have stayed late at the studio with this kind of deadline looming. She and Cooper would have ordered Malaysian food and beer. They would have played loud music— Pearl Jam in the early hours, Coltrane in the late. Eventually they would have gotten looped on exhaustion, and they would have told each other about first lovers or bad bosses or broken hearts, like two girls at a slumber party.

At her portable lightboard, Isabel sighed at this thought. Anna looked up from her painting, then went back to it. And Isabel forced herself to concentrate, to go back to her work. It was exacting collage work, the kind everybody did on the computer these days. But she wanted a certain effect, one she had mastered a long time ago and didn't trust to Photo-Shop.

After a while, Anna sighed. Then she muttered bitterly. Isabel thought it might even have been a curse word, one Anna had heard from her, no doubt. The girl was looking at her painting in complete disgust.

Isabel got up and crossed the room in her silent stocking feet. "What's the problem?" she asked, kneeling down next to Luke's daughter.

"Nothin'," Anna said.

"What?"

Anna sighed again. "I can't get the leaves to look real."

Isabel looked at the painting, a scene from Central Park, quite accomplished really, in a primitive way. She could see immediately how to fix it. But she didn't know how that would fly with Anna, her interference. The girl was allergic to her after all, probably allergic to any of her suggestions too. Still, it was worth a try . . . "Mind if I give it a shot?"

Anna paused, thinking about it. She shrugged finally. "I already screwed it up anyway."

Isabel took over the paintbrush and dipped it in orange watercolor. She began dabbing and swishing individual bits of orange on the balloonlike tree Anna had painted. With each stroke, she made a *shh-shh* sound. The tree became a tree.

Anna said, "Cool." And leaned closer, really studied the technique. "Where'd you learn that?"

Isabel shrugged and smiled. "Took some art classes when I was at NYU." She pushed the drawing back to Anna. "Here. You try."

Anna took back the drawing and began using the same technique, a little tentatively.

Isabel said, "It helps if you make the little *shh-shh*."

Anna began making the little *shh-shh* noise as she painted away, absorbedly.

This made Isabel smile. She turned to go back to her light table, to her own project.

"Hey," Anna said.

Isabel turned.

Anna eked out a tiny smile, so tiny. "Thanks," she said, just the way her mother had taught her.

Isabel smiled back and nodded. She would take what she could get. She would take that tiniest of smiles.

JACKIE

She had stayed up late in the sewing room, working until she felt the hour burning in her eyeballs, throbbing. It always happened that way, her ambition outstripped her time and energy. But, this year of all years, she was not going to disappoint the children. And so when Isabel had dropped them home that morning, their costumes had been ready. Ben had taken one look, and cried, "It's just what I wanted. It's just what I wanted." He had tried to climb Jackie like a tree, just to kiss her.

Ben's fantasy costume was a bunny suit coming out of a top hat, as though he were a magician's trick. And Anna was Elvis Presley in gold lamé and a high stiff puff. Even her lip seemed to curl when she was wearing it.

Jackie took cutout pumpkin cookies to the school parade, then she walked home with them through the neighborhood so that they could trick-or-treat. It was the perfect Halloween evening. The trees were half-bare, and the leaves skittered by on the wind. Jackie thought, *If there has to be a last . . .*

And then she stopped herself. She feared that her body could be swayed by her mind. She was on constant guard against dread, against letting herself consider the worst. She had to be on guard.

Ben was with his friends, racing three squares ahead on the sidewalk, but Anna stayed back with her mother. She was in a confiding mood, Mommy's little Elvis. Anna said, "I've been thinking . . . about what you said about Isabel. You know, how we should see the good side of her . . ."

Jackie nodded.

"And you're right. I mean, she knows all about clothes and stuff, and every rock-and-roll song ever written. She's still like a kid herself."

Jackie fought to keep her face from showing what she really felt, which was a sudden misgiving, a sudden shifting of the sidewalk under her feet. Carefully, she watched each step she took and tried to find it in herself to reward her daughter for listening to her mother on the subject of Isabel, for heeding her own advice. But inside Jackie something was crumpling, something vital to her. "Like a big sister," she said, minimizing.

Anna nodded. "She knows every neat junk-food place," she said. "Actually, she's kind of cool. When you get to know her."

"I bet," Jackie said evenly. She could feel Anna watching her. Did her daughter know her so well that she could sense her turmoil? Did it shimmer off her flesh in vibrations? Did it have some scent that would betray her?

No, because when Anna spoke again, it was only to say, "But don't tell her I told you."

It turned out, her daughter's only concern was that Isabel not find out that Anna was softening toward her. Anna was only interested in protecting her own tentative feelings. Not her mother's.

"Secret's safe with me," Jackie said. But she herself felt unsafe, suddenly exposed and imperiled. Even her Anna was warming to Isabel.

ISABEL

On Thursday afternoon, she was on the road again, ferrying the kids up to Nyack. Luke had picked the kids up after school for a quick couple of hours with them before he went off to Pittsburgh again. He said he wouldn't do it if she didn't have the time to take them back up to Jackie because he knew Isabel's schedule was too jammed to keep them for the night and, anyway, Jackie wanted them. And how could Isabel say no to him? Then Luke wouldn't get to see his kids at all until next Tuesday. So here she was. Late.

Isabel could remember when her life ran on a cord between the studio and her apartment. She was either en route one way or the other, sliding, sliding, sliding. Her days had a predictably harried quality, but there were only those two destinations. Simple. Anything else was a spur trip, an impulse. And now she was a chauffeur darting up and down the Hudson with precious cargo: dashing to mesh with soccer schedules, with riding lessons, with seventh-birthday parties. It was her fault of course. Early on, when she thought it might still make a difference in the way someone felt about her— Luke? Jackie? the kids?—she had volunteered for this kind of duty. But now, often, it just felt like it was expected of her. And it felt thankless.

She turned up the radio. Unexpectedly, Anna shot a pleased look at her, almost a grin. The song was "Ain't No Mountain High Enough." Isabel started singing and to her surprise, Anna joined in. Finally Ben's voice came from the back, his spindly, rubber-band voice blending with the music that filled the car.

She smiled at the kids; they smiled back.

Duncan was expecting Isabel for a client meeting tonight, drinks at the Plaza. She hated giving up her evenings, but with Luke away, she might as well. It wouldn't hurt to appease Duncan. He needed as much coddling as most boyfriends. It was a sick relationship. But it was a great career.

Using the rearview mirror, she put on some makeup. The mascara was the real challenge, and she noticed that Anna was watching her carefully from the passenger seat. The blush just brushed right on. The lipstick was simple, too. She was never one to wear much makeup. Grandma Celie had told her it would give her pimples, and she had shied away. Since then, she had used it only when she had to. She'd gone all day without it today, but Duncan would kill her if she turned up looking like she wasn't turned out. She put on a darker shade of gloss, for low light.

Anna was still watching her. After she pressed her lips together, Isabel passed the tube to Anna. The girl paused a minute. Then she took it. She even managed a little smile in exchange.

Maybe, Isabel thought then. *Maybe finally . . .*

Right now, her errand didn't feel so thankless after all.

At Jackie's house, she followed the kids inside. Anna ran straight to show her mother the lip gloss. Isabel tried to stop her, but it was too late. "Mom, look what Isabel gave me."

Jackie studied her daughter, and Isabel could see the look soak into Anna's enthusiasm. The girl said, "It's not to wear around or anything. I'm way too young. It's just for play."

Isabel hated that smile of Jackie's, that taut smile that didn't give warmth, only judgment. She hated it more when Jackie quipped, "That is so pretty. You usually only see that color on working girls."

So Isabel had no choice but to glare at her.

Jackie said to Ben, "You are a lucky boy, you get to watch a video tonight. With Colleen." He beamed, then she turned back to Anna, and said, "We have to leave in ten minutes."

"Huh?"

"We're going out."

"Where?" Anna was clearly intrigued.

Jackie whipped out two concert tickets and gave them to Anna, who examined them. Her face lighted up. "Pearl Jam!"

"Fifth row. Center."

"Wow, Mom, you are the coolest."

Isabel thought her anger would explode out of her. It was like a tiny bubble in her stomach that was expanding and expanding. Of all the mean things . . .

Jackie was hugging her daughter, stroking her head. "Well," she said, "I thought . . . it's been a while since I've been to a mosh pit." It was intended more for Isabel than Anna. It was Isabel's eyes she held.

Anna turned to Isabel now, and said, "Is my mom the greatest, or what?"

Isabel managed a smile. At least she thought she did. She nodded and agreed. "The greatest." But inside she was thinking, *Maybe not . . . not with Jackie in the middle. Maybe never.*

JACKIE

As if a Pearl Jam concert hadn't been torture enough for one week, now Jackie had to endure chemo. She had told the doctor that tonight was no good. It was spaghetti-and-meatballs night, and Ben counted on it. But Dr. Sweikert had given her a look that said, in no uncertain terms, that the beginning of chemotherapy trumped spaghetti and meatballs. So here she was in a hospital bed with the best nighttime view of Manhattan she had ever had: It was as though the city was constructed of strung lights, no substance, no support, only light suspended in darkness. And she had to get cancer to see the city this way.

The chemo came in a Walkman. Or that's what it looked like to Jackie. Dr. Sweikert had managed a small smile when Jackie had asked jokingly if it had headphones. It didn't. It contained a day's dose of the drugs, automatically released into her bloodstream every twenty minutes, and it was so lightweight, she could wear it everywhere. "To jog," the doctor said. "Or play tennis. It stays hidden under your clothes."

The surgical team had created a shunt at her collarbone, a small mouth in her skin that would gulp in the chemicals. It was like having an electrical outlet installed on her body. But she had to agree with the doctor that it was a preferred alternative to the more traditional treatment, which was four hours in the hospital once a week with an IV stuck in her arm. And this way, the side effects were minimal. Dr. Sweikert had explained that on certain days Jackie would have some nausea, some drowsiness. Other days would be good.

"Hair loss?" Jackie had asked.

"Maybe. Maybe not."

She would live with it either way. Or maybe die with it. She touched that thought. More and more it was unavoidable. She was like a child worrying a scab.

And now it was over, the surgery. She was plugged into a Walkman. There were chemicals coursing in her that were powerful enough to kill cells, to kill her if the balance were wrong. She did not feel sick so much. She felt lonely.

Her pager went off. Luke's number at the loft. It would be the kids, probably wondering what was up and why she wasn't with them on spaghetti-and-meatball night, probably wondering why they had to eat Luke's penne with artichoke hearts and capers—again.

She dialed. Ben answered. His voice was silver as the light outside her window, spun silver, she thought. "Mom," he cried, "you're not gonna believe it."

"What?"

"I'm tele-pathetic," he said.

"You mean telepathic?"

"That's what I said. I just discovered it today. I can read minds. I just tried it with Dad and Isabel, and guess what? I always knew exactly what they were thinking."

"That's incredible, honey."

"Want me to read yours?"

"Sure. Go ahead."

His voice got grave and serious. "Think real hard about something."

Jackie sat with her eyes out the window, wishing that she was out among those lights, that she was downtown picking him up, that he was reading her mind in person. "I'm thinking," she told him.

"Concentrate." She could hear the concentration in his voice. He was coaching himself as much as her.

"I am."

Silence hung on the connection. Then, after a long pause, he said, with some satisfaction, "You're thinking about me."

"Wow!" she told him. "That's right. What else?"

"You're wishing you were here instead of where you are."

Tears swelled in her throat, in her eyes. "Right again."

"Where are you anyway?" he asked.

"In bed. I've got a flu bug. You know, I'm turning green. Barfing."

"I knew that," he assured her. "And you're wishing you were making me spaghetti so I wouldn't have to eat Daddy's sucky lamb chops." He whispered the last part.

In her bed, she smiled and bit down on the tears. "You got that right."

"See? I'm patho-telic."

"Telepathic.

"That's what I said."

She closed her eyes, wishing for him all the things she had always wished for him—for summers at the lake in Maine and for confidence in his schoolwork and later his professional life, for rainy mornings when he could sleep in and for pristine mornings when he could climb out of bed to watch the sun rise over the Grand Canyon or the ocean or his backyard swing. She wished him a father and a mother and a sister. She wished him happiness and health. She wished him all the things she could not give him, could never guarantee him. She wished them true.

"Mommy," he said. "When are you coming home?"

"In the morning."

"Oh," he said, the disappointment whispering along the words. "I wanted to see you tonight."

She bit her lip. Then she said brightly, too brightly, "We can still see each other."

"We can?"

"Mmmhmm. We'll do what we always do." What they had always done since there had been nights when he didn't sleep in his bedroom down the hall, nights when she couldn't get up and go listen to his breathing, nights when he had a daddy living somewhere else and he had to go somewhere else, too. "We'll meet someplace special," she told him. "In our dreams."

"Cool," he said. "Where this time?"

"Disneyland?" That had always been a favorite with him.

"Naw. Last time the lines were too long."

She smiled at this feat of his imagination. "The beach?" she suggested.

"Yeah," he enthused, "on a hot summer day."

"With giant waves."

"And boogie boards."

"And corn dogs," she said.

"Awesome," he told her.

"See you there," she whispered into the phone. "Put on plenty of lotion."

"It's a dream, Mom. You don't need lotion."

Her eyes filled with tears. They spilled over. But she tried to keep the sound of them out of her voice.

"Mommy?" he asked. "You still there?"

She wiped away the tears as they came. "Yeah, baby, I'm here."

"I gotta go. See you later. Bye."

"Bye, sweetie. I'll see you in my dreams." And then she lay there with the tears running out of her closed eyes and tried to find the way into sleep, the way to the beach where Ben would be waiting and there would be waves and sunshine and boogie boards and where there would be no Walkman and no shunt and no cancer.

ISABEL

The soccer game was in full swing when Isabel arrived. She could see Luke on the sidelines, coaching. (His butt looked cute, and she'd have to give him a squeeze later and remind him of that fact.) Anna was on the field, grim as a soldier. Isabel scanned the bleachers for Ben and saw only Jackie, looking pale and tired. Well, she had no choice. She wasn't going to snub the children's mother in front of all their friends and neighbors, in front of the whole town of Nyack, New York. She took the steps two at a time and swung herself into the empty seat next to Jackie.

Jackie looked away from the field, saw that it was Isabel. She nodded hello, then scanned the playground area where Ben was climbing on the jungle gym and plastic-swordfighting with his buddies. Even sitting here at a kids' soccer game, Jackie was all business. There were things to be done, accounting to be kept.

Isabel focused on the action down on the field. She had never been much of a sports fan. She liked sports. It was simply that she liked participating in them. Watching didn't offer the same thrill—no adrenaline, no sweat, no cold beer well earned. Her eyes followed Anna. She was chasing the ball down the field. Her hair was hanging down over her eyes. Isabel pointed this out to Jackie.

Jackie nodded. "It means she's avoiding a confrontation."

Isabel turned to Jackie, interested.

Jackie actually continued talking. "If she's twirling her hair, she's playing something out in her mind. If she's stopped combing it, she's depressed."

Anna was like a book that Jackie read, Isabel thought. She wondered if all mothers did that, if her own had ever known things about her that she didn't know about herself. She would never know now. There was no one to ask that sort of thing, no one who might remember such an intimate little fact from a long time ago. Isabel asked Jackie, "What about obsessively picking her split ends?"

"Anxiety."

"Last week when she chopped her Barbie bangs all to hell . . . ?"

"She was angry at herself."

"Jackie?"

Jackie looked at her. "Yes?"

"When I twist my hair like this, it means I'm worried sick about something."

Jackie's mouth twitched into a slight smile. But it was a smile. "I'll keep it in mind. And use it against you." She turned to look back at the game, at Anna behind her hair, avoiding confrontation.

Isabel kept watching Jackie's profile. "You feeling all right?" she asked.

Without turning, Jackie said, "Me? I'm fine. Great."

"You look tired."

"I hate when people say that. It's a nice way of telling someone they look like shit."

"No."

Jackie shrugged. "I've just got things on my mind. You know."

Isabel didn't know. What things? But she had a guess. "Are you seeing someone?"

Jackie snorted a laugh. "I wish that was the reason I was tired. Actually, I'm . . . Well, I'm . . ." She paused. Isabel had never seen her at a loss for words. She was an editor after all, a wordsmith. She seemed to be sorting between options, choosing carefully between vocabulary words. "I'm thinking of going back to Random House."

"Wow," Isabel said. "That's wonderful. Great."

Jackie's eyes never left the soccer field. "Yeah, and while I'm working it out with the editorial director, I'll need to make some trips into the city. Sometimes very late."

"Hey, any help you need, we'll cover." Her own generosity even surprised Isabel. Not that she had an impulse to it, that was just the way she was; she invariably gave a single to any homeless person who showed her a cup. But that she had any generosity left for Jackie Harrison, that was the shocker. Maybe it was just by virtue of the fact that Jackie was actually speaking with her for once, even confiding. Being civil.

Jackie nodded her appreciation at the offer. But she still didn't turn to look Isabel in the eye.

Isabel said, "Have you told Luke and the kids?"

Now, Jackie turned to her with hard eyes. Her

voice was heavy with seriousness. "No," she said. "I want to hold off for a bit. It may not happen. Our secret, okay?"

"Sure," Isabel said, shrugging. "If you like."

Jackie swept her gaze back toward the playground. Ben was clinging to a high cage on the jungle gym, fencing with another boy. He wasn't paying enough attention to how high he was, to hanging on. "Ben, be careful . . ." Jackie muttered.

And then, in a blink, he slipped. He fell. It seemed like forever that he was in the air. His body crumpled when it hit, and he lay motionless.

Isabel seemed to be pulled by the same cord that propelled Jackie. Shoulder to shoulder, they raced down the bleachers and broke out across the grass. Isabel's mind whirled with possibilities. She strained to see Ben move, if he was okay. She pulled out ahead of Jackie, raced ahead.

When she got close enough to see that he was holding his leg, when she got close enough that she could have reached for him, she stopped. She let Jackie pass her by and kneel at his side. She stood back as Luke arrived, and as Jackie lifted Ben. There was blood. His pants were torn; his knee was torn. "Mommy," he said through his pain, "can I still go to Tucker's party tomorrow?"

That's when Isabel started feeling better. That's when she relearned the reflex of breathing.

Afterward, following Luke's car, which was following Jackie's car to the hospital, Isabel felt strangely calm. Jackie had known just what to do, just how to handle him. But Isabel had known, too. She had been there, stride for stride, heartbeat for heartbeat. She had known what only mothers knew. It was inside her, too.

Ben needed five stitches, and Isabel and Luke stayed with him while Jackie haggled over the insurance papers. It was in her name. It was her responsibility, and the receptionist rebuffed Luke's effort to take over so the boy's mother could hold Ben while he got stitched up. In fact, Jackie still wasn't there when the doctor had finished and Ben was propped up on pillows like some boy king, eating chocolate pudding that Isabel spooned up for him.

Luke left to go find Jackie.

Isabel picked up Ben's hand. She said, "I'm proud of you. You were very brave."

"Didn't hurt that bad," he said. "Besides, it'll be pretty cool to show my friends." He studied his injury, trying to gauge its wow-factor. "Hey," he said. "Would you do me a favor?"

"Maybe. Depends on what it is." He was going to be okay. He was already back to negotiating. It was his daddy's genes in him.

"Will you ask Dad to get me a white dove for Christmas?"

"We'll see."

"Come on, please. Every magician needs a white dove. A real one. They do."

"It's a long way off. We'll talk to your mom, okay?"

He nodded, then moved his leg too much. In pain, he grabbed it. "Ow, it's startin' to hurt."

She knew just what to do. She hugged him, comforting him, and she began to sing a song she didn't know she remembered, a song she couldn't even remember hearing for the first time because she had always heard it. It was a song that had always made her feel better, and one that now made her want to cry. From happiness. There was something of her mother still in her.

JACKIE

She was having trouble with the laundry. Bending to get the clothes from the kids' baskets made her dizzy. Colors burst before her eyes, spread and dissolved. Her hand shook so much that she couldn't measure the detergent into a cup. It spilled directly into the basin, swirling in. When she finally got the kids' play clothes going in a cold-water wash, she stood bent over the machine with her forehead pressed against the cool vibration. It made her feel some better. But afterward all her strength was necessary to get the dryer door open, and she had to sit on the floor to fold the whites—Ben's tee shirts and Anna's undies and her own pillowcases. Last night had been hard; she had drenched the pillowcases, with sweat and tears.

The nausea surged up now and tugged at the base of her tongue, and she didn't feel equal to the effort of standing. So she crawled to the basement bathroom and knelt by the toilet, hung on. It was the fourth time today she had thrown up, and the muscles knitted along her ribs ached from it. It was worse for her because it felt like sobbing. And noticing this triggered a sob. And the sob made her disgusted with herself.

There had been other bad days, days when the

waves of nausea had washed around in her, sloshed. There had been other days when her hands trembled and her knee joints seemed made of rubber. And then she had gone to sit in the Adirondack chairs on the lawn. She had lifted her face to the sunshine and chewed crystallized ginger until her tongue burned. It had been merely a sickness of flesh. Today, it was partly a sickness of spirit.

All because she had caught Isabel singing to Ben the day before. Hurrying to get back to her injured son, she had raced up to his hospital door—only to be struck still. Isabel's voice reached her first, and then she had dared to look. Her son was rapt, and Jackie had seen instantly the easy affection between Ben and Isabel. She had seen the truth: Isabel cared about her children. Isabel did not merely love Luke, she loved his children. Jackie had stood paralyzed beyond the door of Ben's room, paralyzed by reality, and she had heard Isabel singing that song to her little son, and afterward she could not forget the sound of it. Last night, fighting for sleep, Isabel's voice had sung in her head like some tormenting Greek chorus. It was such an old-fashioned song for someone to sing, someone so young, and yet Isabel had sung it so soulfully, as if she might know what it meant. And how could she know anything about leaving? About needing?

Jackie pulled herself up and sat on the closed toilet seat. She knew this was craziness: to begrudge her children the love of their father's next wife. It was foolishness. Her children might need that love. They might need it more than anything.

But she could not bear to think this way. She couldn't allow it. Standing, Jackie walked to the laundry room and picked up the basket of folded laundry. It must be getting late by now. She would have to get herself together—a shower, fresh clothes, a hit of a joint if that's what it would take to settle her stomach. She had to push herself a little. It was surely almost time to pick Ben up from Tucker's party. Almost time.

She trudged up the stairs, twice stopping to rest. At the top, when the nausea overwhelmed her again, she spilled the basket of folded laundry and barely made it to the powder room off the front hall. Five times. This made five times.

Her face in the mirror was green, as though she were looking at her reflection in pond water. She turned on the tap and cupped water in her palms and brought it up to her eyelids. She tried to wash color back into her cheeks. It did not work.

Where were her car keys?

Shoving clothes back into the capsized basket, she picked it up. Then she set it back down. The muscles in her arms felt as though they weren't attached to each other in the proper ways. Her legs were not much better. She made it to the chair by the foyer table, sat down heavily. Her keys were lying there. She picked them up, and they rattled against each other, the sound of her tremors.

She closed her eyes. *Jackie*, she said to herself soothingly, like a mother in her head, *Jackie*. Was she sympathizing or scolding? Was she simply trying to call herself back, her true self, the strong one. This wasn't the cancer's fault, nor the chemo's: this sickness. This was her doing, down deep. She remembered reading, in a college psych class, about a woman who was nauseated by libraries. Every time she went into one, she grew faint and had to rush away. But it wasn't because the woman couldn't stand books, it was because she wanted them too much. It was because she wanted the knowledge inside them, and where could she begin? Where could she begin that would ever, ever work her all the way to the end? It was impossible.

It was as impossible as it was for Jackie to have everything she wanted of Anna and Ben. She was greedy for them, for the moment when Anna opened her eyes from sleep and for the moment Ben slurped in a long strand of spaghetti, for the moment when Anna came in at bedtime to snuggle with a book but really to talk and for the moment when Ben emerged from his bath with damp hair and powdery skin. Jackie wanted those moments. She wanted them every time they happened, every chance. Even having them on Mondays, Wednesdays, and Fridays, plus alternate weekends, this was not enough. She wanted all their moments forever. She wanted the moment when Anna would be awarded her diploma, when Ben would slip a ring on his bride. She wanted to watch Anna with her new baby's fingers wrapped around her pinky. Jackie wanted nothing less.

And she could not have it. Even if she lived a life that stretched over nine or ten decades, she could not have all of their moments. Of course she had known that from the beginning. It had made her cry the morning Anna was born, and it had made her cry on subsequent lonely midnights when she could not sleep. She had known . . .

But this disease, this cancer had made the fact her faithful companion. It was as attached to her as her chemo Walkman: *Never enough. Never enough.*

She knew minute by minute that live now or die now, it was never going to be enough. Jackie was always going to be like the woman surrounded by books that made her sick because she desired them so much. Jackie was sick with what she wanted and couldn't have. You could call it cancer, or chemotherapy. But it was more than that. What she felt right now was more than cancer or chemotherapy.

Seeing Isabel share a moment that should have been her own with Ben, that is what had made Jackie sick today. It had weakened her with a complicated cocktail of emotions. This cocktail was as blended as the chemicals that coursed through her, seeking out the flawed cancer cells. This cocktail was seeking out the flaw in her heart that resisted what was best. She knew that her children needed Isabel to love them. She knew that it was for the best. Especially if . . .

But they were her children. Hers. Her babies. This was her true weakness, the flaw in her heart: How much she loved them. How highly she placed her love above anyone else's.

She opened her eyes. It was time to go. No time now for a shower, even to change clothes. She lifted the keys. They shook. They clanked.

She lowered them back to her knee.

She could not drive like this. She might harm herself. She might harm Ben. Even Jackie could see, she was out of choices. Even she could see that it was not possible for her to drive, not like this: Someone else would have to go after Ben at Tucker's. And who was she going to call, the president of the PTA, whose calls she screened? Was she going to disturb Colleen from her painting and send

ISABEL

The call came at the studio. Isabel could tell by Cooper's expression who it was. Even Duncan could tell by Cooper's expression who it was. He threw up his hands before Isabel ever even picked up the line. Sure enough, it was Jackie. With no warning whatsoever, here at the last minute—literally the last minute—Jackie reeled off this saga about how she had to be at Random House so she couldn't pick up Ben at Tucker's party. Could Isabel?

Isabel chewed the inside of her lip. The party was fifteen minutes away from Jackie's house but thirty (in perfect traffic) for Isabel to pick Ben up and then drop him off in Nyack. She looked at Duncan, who was vigorously shaking his head: no way. She said, "Okay." Duncan looked like he wanted to grab her by the throat.

But how could Isabel shrug it off? Luke had flown out first thing this morning on the shuttle for DC. And Ben couldn't just walk home. And anyway, after what had happened at the playground, she wouldn't mind seeing that the kid was okay. She'd woken thinking about him this morning, worrying. So she was happy to do it for Ben.

As she was going out the door, Duncan reminded her that she was supposed to help him schmooze these British guys who were shopping a big account. "Okay, okay," she said. "I'll be back." She made it sound like the Terminator, and she thought it was a pretty good mimic of Schwarzenegger. But Duncan didn't laugh. He wasn't laughing much these days.

The traffic was spastic. Some days it seemed like every driver in New York was playing bumper cars, racing up to the next guy's bumper, then slotting over into the next lane and then back again. It drove her nuts. She was smacking her gum like a madwoman, and this annoyed her even more. Rolling down the window, she threw out her gum—and the directions to Tucker's birthday party accidentally blew out with it.

"Dammit," she said, striking the wheel. Now what was she going to do?

She picked up the phone and got directory assistance to give her the number for Random House. She got transferred to a man. She said, "Hi, I'm looking for Jackie Harrison. I'm supposed to pick up her kids from a birthday party. I know the street name . . . But I lost the house number. If I could just speak with her . . ."

"I'm sorry," the man interrupted. "Ms. Harrison is not here."

"But she said she's been meeting with the editorial director for the last . . ."

"Miss, I am the editorial director. I haven't seen Ms. Harrison since she left Random House eleven years ago."

"What?" she stammered. "But . . . hmm . . .

Well, thank you for your time." She was completely baffled.

"Balloons," the editorial director said, before she could hang up.

"Pardon?"

"Just look for a house with balloons. Never fails. The kids will be there."

And Ben was there. Isabel did find him at the house with balloons strung on the fence post. The little squeaker had chocolate smeared down the front of his shirt. And he was definitely on some kind of sugar high. He chattered the whole way to Jackie's, and Isabel was sure he was going to spill his loot bag or lose the souvenir balloons out the window or dump over the wedge of cake that Tucker's mom had wrapped for him to take home. All of which would be just fine, would be normal Ben-behavior, and no big deal, if Isabel weren't ticked off: Jackie had out-and-out lied to her.

Jackie obviously thought she could just manipulate her with lies, get Isabel to do her errands on any old whim. And, when Isabel pulled into the Nyack driveway, her peevishness spiked. There was Jackie sitting in an Adirondack chair, wrapped in a blanket and reading the mail: cozy as could be.

Ben rushed ahead to his mother, while Isabel tried to juggle his loot. She heard Jackie say, "Look at you." And then the two of them disappeared into the house to stick the shirt in the laundry. *Anal*, Isabel thought. *Can't let her kid stay dirty for ten seconds.*

She looked for a place to put down Ben's party goodies and ended up balancing them on the table that held Jackie's mail. And she couldn't help noticing the mail. There was an airline ticket from JFK to Los Angeles, and tucked inside it was a folded fax. She knew she shouldn't, but she did anyway: She opened it. The letterhead was from Random House in California. It read, "Jackie, Can't wait to see you here. I know you're anxious. But it's going to be wonderful. Everything will work out perfectly. I promise. Till then, Charlie."

Oh my God, Isabel realized. *Jackie is moving to L.A.* And then the porch door squeaked, and Isabel panicked because she was totally being a snoop. She hurriedly replaced everything she had been poking through. When she looked up, Jackie was coming toward her. Jackie asked, "Did you have any trouble with my directions? I got in the car to go into the city for my meeting, and it wouldn't start. Volvos, you know. So did you have any trouble?"

"Nope. None at all." God, Isabel felt so guilty, but how could Jackie plan some life-changing thing like that, and not tell Luke? Or her kids? How could she just upend everything for everybody without so much as a word in warning?

"Well, thanks," Jackie said, brusquely picking up Ben's things from the party. Her body language all but opened the gate for Isabel, all but walked her to the car and waved her off.

Isabel nodded: Jackie was welcome. Sort of.

Jackie turned to go back into the house, back to her son. She seemed so smug and self-contained in her hidden schemes. And suddenly Isabel couldn't help herself. She couldn't let Jackie get away with it. She was too ticked off. "I know your secret," she said, as if the words were a lasso that would wrap around Jackie's neck, hold her there.

Jackie did freeze.

Isabel regretted it then. Instantly. Even before Jackie pivoted to face her, she regretted having opened her mouth. She should have just gone home and waited for Luke to fly in on the shuttle, and she should have told him what she had seen, let him handle it his way. She should not have acted on her own pique at being used like a pawn by his ex-wife. But she had to keep going now. Jackie was standing there, facing her down. Isabel said, "I saw the airline tickets, and the note from your new boss."

Jackie said, "My boss." Nothing more.

Isabel felt goaded on by this nonresponse. "You're not working at Random House in New York. I talked to them."

Jackie spat out, "You what?"

Isabel squared her shoulders. "You're taking the kids, and moving to Los Angeles." There, she had said it. She had said the truth that Jackie wanted to hide—and had no right to hide.

It wasn't an explosion that followed. It was eerily quiet fury. "What the hell do you think you're doing? Reading my mail, snooping around behind my back like some dishonest little . . ."

"Dishonest?" Isabel said pointedly. "I wouldn't have to snoop around if you were honest with the father of your children."

Jackie measured Isabel with a long look, left her suspended in the silence that she always used as her most eloquent tool. There was something of surprise in her face though. Suddenly Jackie seemed not only angry but taken aback. She said, "I'd have thought this was the answer to your prayers. Lose the witch and her two brats. In one swoop. Simplifies everything. You'll have your life back."

"Come on," Isabel said, thinking of poor Luke, of never seeing the children except on alternate holidays and some weeks in the summer. "There are so many publishing houses in New York. Surely you could find one here."

Jackie's steeliness returned. "If you're so goddamn concerned about this, why don't you change careers? Why don't you and Luke move to L.A.? Because I am sick of accommodating your schedules and rearranging my life." Jackie's voice was stretched thin, strained by feeling.

But Isabel had her own feelings about this. Who was accommodating whose schedule, and who was rearranging whose life? She had her own anger on this subject. She vented it. "So you make plans to rearrange everyone else's life without consulting us?" she asked.

"Bicoastal parenting," Jackie said with a nonchalance Isabel knew she couldn't really mean. Not Jackie Harrison, Quintessential PTA-Certified Good Mother. "Happens every day. Luke gets the kids every other summer. Every other holiday. It's not ideal. But people make it work."

Jackie was toying with her, Isabel knew. She didn't mean that. She was poking at her with that idea, as though it were a sharp stick. She wanted a reaction.

Isabel tried to give her only an honest one. "You can't do that. You can't take Luke's children away from him. We can't live like that."

"We?" Jackie asked, as if Isabel didn't count, as if hauling her kids around and getting them up for school and helping them with their school assignments, as if all of that counted for nothing. Jackie said dismissively, "You let Luke talk to me if he has a problem with this. This doesn't concern you. We don't need you to solve our problems."

"It's my problem, too," Isabel countered. If no one else was going to recognize it, she was going to point it out. Jackie could condescend to her all she wanted, but she was at least going to hear that Isabel had some weight in this decision.

"Oh?"

"I am going to marry this man. And we are going to have a life together." She tried to speak calmly. She tried to let the honesty of her feelings speak for itself. Surely Jackie could understand, she thought. Surely Jackie had once loved Luke enough to understand how Isabel loved him, how she didn't want him to be hurt. "I love him," she said. "And these kids are his life. He'd be devastated not to be near them. It's just . . . Jackie, please." She felt helpless in front of this woman, try as she might to muster an argument. Words failed her, the right words. She felt so much but could say so little. "Please."

Jackie's face changed. It was just a series of twitches that did it, just a few muscles rearranging themselves. It was hardly noticeable, except that the two of them were looking at one another intently. So Isabel saw it immediately. She heard how Jackie's voice came out differently, then, too, as though it were being dragged across something that shredded it. "You're a moron, kid," Jackie said quietly. "You guessed the wrong secret."

Isabel waited, feeling a tremendous uncertainty.

She didn't know what to expect now, if she ever had. But ferocity she could deal with, was accustomed to dealing with from Jackie, also hostility and condescension and iciness. She couldn't read what she was getting off Jackie now. She only knew that she had seen the airline tickets with her own pair of eyes. How could she be wrong about that?

After a long taut pause, Jackie sat down in one of the Adirondack chairs, and it seemed a signal of surrender, some kind of surrender. She started to light a joint—Jackie Harrison lighting a joint? Isabel could see that her hands were shaking. Jackie said, "Charlie Drummond used to be a colleague at Random House in New York. She moved to the West Coast office. So I'm gonna crash at her place, while I take some new protein injections my *oncologist* recommended. I can only get them in Los Angeles."

The skin reacted on Isabel's neck even before she was conscious of beginning to understand. "Oncologist?" she echoed.

Jackie took a long hit of the joint, offered it to Isabel, who shook her head no. Jackie explained, "It takes the edge off the nausea." She attempted a smile, one of her wry, annoying Jackie smiles. But she didn't quite pull it off, not in its full vigor. "Life's a trade-off. It's finally legal to smoke dope, but you gotta have cancer."

Cancer? Isabel was trying to breathe. It felt like something physical that she had to swallow. It went down hard.

She had been so wrong. So wrong. And now she was scared, suddenly so scared of what might happen to Jackie and to her children, to Luke, and before she knew it, before she could help herself,

Isabel had asked what adults should never ask, she had asked like a child, "Are you dying?"

The children's mother didn't flinch though, even diminished as she was by having to admit her secret, by having to admit it to Isabel of all people. "Not today," she said.

LUKE

He was famished. He had rushed to the airport to make the earlier shuttle, as a surprise for Isabel. They had had so little time together in the past weeks, what with his competing cases in Pittsburgh and DC, plus his various family obligations. The two of them hadn't even celebrated their engagement properly. You certainly couldn't count a beer toast after one of Anna's soccer games as a suitable celebration of the fact that Isabel had agreed to spend the rest of her life waking up next to him. Maybe she'd be home already, he thought as the limo crossed the bridge into Manhattan, and they could sneak out to Antoine's. She always loved that. Sometimes he thought she loved it more than his cooking—because of the nostalgia factor. "Isabella," the staff always cried when she walked in the front door of the restaurant.

The car dropped him at the building, and even as he was shutting the door, Luke looked up to see if the lights were on. Yes. She was home. He smiled. His girl.

"I'm home," he called merrily into the loft.

He waited for her smile.

It didn't come. She came around the corner and

into his arms, but her face was wet. She looked bruised.

"What is it?" he demanded.

"You have to see Jackie," she said. "Immediately."

"The kids?" His heart lurched inside him. What had happened to Anna or Ben?

She shook her head. "They're okay. Call Jackie. Make her see you."

He studied her. "Why? What's happened now?"

"I can't . . ." Isabel said. "Call Jackie."

He did, and Jackie put up no fight. He ate a banana in the car driving up and rifled through possibilities in his head. Was something up with the school? But, no, what could have unhinged Isabel? Had his ex-wife gone to the lawyer, as she had threatened? Was she getting his custody revoked? Jackie hadn't sounded spiteful on the phone. She had just stipulated that she would meet him at the tavern, not at the house. Colleen would come over and entertain the kids.

Actually, he was relieved when he walked into the tavern and saw Jackie waiting for him. He was relieved because her face bore none of the same horror as Isabel's. Even her words, when she told him her news, didn't correspond with her cool Jackieness, her solidity, her presence: Invoking the possibility of her own absence seemed preposterous. Not Jackie. She had such tenacity.

Cancer? the word sounded in him like a gong. It wouldn't stop echoing. It had a vibration.

"Are you sure?" he had asked. "How can you be sure?"

"The x-rays confirmed it," she said, "and the

MRI. The doctors all agree." She went on to say that she had had a lump removed from her breast the year before, so small she hadn't wanted to bother him with it.

"Bother me?" he asked her. And then he asked himself if he had pushed her that far away, if he had done this, isolated her dangerously. He of all people understood her tendency to live in solitude, to brace herself away from all but those most essential to her heart. Looking back, he could see that he had told himself that she was the one shoving him out of her life. But he was the one who had ignored the vulnerability under her actions, under her words. He had gone. Just gone. He had never tried to stay close enough to know what she might need of him still. He had walked. And now here she was . . .

She explained that the doctors last year thought they had it all. Only now it was back. Now it had spread into some lymph nodes, into other organs. Its potential had grown. Jackie might be solid and present. But the facts were as well. He kept staring at his clenched hands, trying to understand.

He felt her watching him. "I know," she said finally. "I wouldn't know what to say either . . . if it were you."

He looked up into her eyes then. He vowed, "We're going to beat this."

She smiled, a quick twitch of a smile, but warm. "Walk in the park. And thanks for the 'we.' "

Tears worked up on him then. But there were no tears in her eyes. She was composure itself.

His voice cracked when he spoke. "You're not alone in this. You're not alone. Okay?" He regretted every angry word that had passed between them. He regretted how the marriage had faltered, how his stamina had failed him. But the only apology he could make was to say, "You're not alone."

He saw her swallow. He saw his words get to her. She tried to smile but looked down instead. It should have been him instead. It should have been. He told her this.

"I'd go along with that," she said. And after a long pause, they managed to swap the smallest of smiles.

Two nights later, when it came to telling the children, she was amazing. She was all smiles. Luke settled in with Ben in the living room, and he could hear Jackie in the kitchen with Anna, making hot cocoa. When they came in together—two girl-friends—Jackie served Ben with a flourish and said, "Thirty-seven marshmallows. Your sister counted them in."

But for all her mother's sunniness, Anna was on alert. Her nerves seemed to give off static electricity. Finally, it was Anna who sliced through the politeness, who sliced through the *trompe l'oeil* of the four of them sitting in the living room, a knife through painted canvas, through the fake family. "So what's up?" she asked. "Who's marrying who this time?"

"Mommy's marrying Isabel," Ben quipped.

Luke had smiled at this. He had smiled because he couldn't find any words to help Jackie, to take the burden that was ultimately hers to pass to them. And anyway she made it look as though she didn't need any help, from him or anyone else. She looked directly at each of the children, from Anna to Ben.

She spoke simply, not gravely. "Mommy's sick, guys."

"You still have the flu?" Ben asked.

"I have cancer."

Just like that. Luke felt his insides jolt at the starkness. She was brave. He had told her this, at the restaurant, and she had said it was because she had been living with it longer.

"Do you know what that is?" she asked the kids.

Ben shook his head. But Anna knew. Her spine had stiffened. She said, "It's what Aunt Mary died from."

This flagged Ben to trouble. His eyes whipped over to Anna. Luke saw him recognize his sister's cold fear. He swung his eyes back to Jackie. She was still solid and calm. She was still smiling. She told them, "Aunt Mary had a different kind. There are lots of kinds. Hers was very bad."

Luke could see the color seeping into his daughter's pale skin, that flush that looked as though it would burn if you touched it. Her face was perfectly still, but the flush gave her away. The acid was loose in her. Anna knew. She understood.

"Is yours bad?" Ben wanted to know.

"Shut up," Anna snapped. "She's going to die." She glared at her mother, so angry.

And Luke felt helpless, noticed his own clenched hands again, always clenched and useless. He wished he could be a magnet, wished he could attract his daughter's anger and spare her mother.

Still, Jackie didn't waver. She didn't acknowledge Anna's outburst. "Actually, I've been working with a doctor for the past few months. To get better. There's every reason to be hopeful that I'm gonna be okay." Her tone gave every reason. She lifted her sweater to show the kids her chemo Walkman. "Check this out," she told them. "It's really cool."

Ben was intrigued. Anna wouldn't even look.

Jackie explained that the Walkman was always giving her medicine, "to fight the disease and make me stronger."

"Can I catch it?" Ben asked. "The cancer?"

Jackie smiled and hugged him to her. "No, honey. It's not contagious."

Anna interrupted their moment. "So you've known about this for a long time?" Her bitterness was an accusation hidden in the question.

Her mother nodded.

"And you never told me."

For the first time, Jackie seemed at a loss. Her eyes glanced off Luke's. She stammered, then gained momentum: "I know how scared I get when you're sick. So I waited to tell you. Until it was getting smaller. I thought that was the best. But I was wrong." Her voice reached for Anna, tried to embrace her. Jackie leaned toward her daughter. "But I promise, from now on, you will *always* know what's going on."

Anna glared at her mother, and Luke wished that he could intercept that look, the slap of it on Jackie's vulnerability, her hidden vulnerability. It surprised him, still surprised him, the cruelty in children, in his Anna. In defense of herself, to protect her most tender needs, his daughter would become instantly vicious. And she was vicious now: "You lied when you never told us. If you lied then, maybe you're lying now." She stood up. "I can never believe you again."

Luke couldn't sit idly now. He said firmly, "Anna, never say never . . ."

Jackie raised her hand to stop him there. Back off, it said. This belonged to her. Meanwhile she never broke eye contact with their daughter. "It was a mistake, Anna. We make mistakes. And we forgive each other. Because we love each other."

Anna whirled away, reckless now, desperate. "Where's Isabel?" she asked.

"What?"

"It's Thursday. We get to be with Isabel. She shoulda picked us up by now." Anna stood like a statue of an angry child. Her shoulders could hold up the world.

"I'd rather be with Mommy," Ben said quietly. Even he was cowed by his sister's fury.

"She's dying," Anna said, turning on him. "Isabel is your mother now." She ran toward the stairs.

Luke had been coiled, but when he saw Jackie's face, when he saw how she was trying to keep hold of herself, of her strength, he felt the spring break. It let loose inside him and drove him to his feet. "Anna!" he screamed.

It startled their daughter. She stopped with her hand clutching the handrail of the stairs.

"You do not run out on your mother," he said.

Anna turned then, so very slowly, and she sent her cruelty straight through him. It pierced to his heart. "Why not?" she asked, staring into his eyes unflinchingly: "You did." And then she climbed the stairs, disappeared from the room. She left the three of them sitting around her fresh absence and his stale absence and the possibility of the worst absence of all.

JACKIE

Jackie searched through the LPs. They were under the turntable in her bedroom, largely forgotten. When Luke had still lived at home, they had moved the turntable up here around the time they got the CD player for downstairs. On Saturday nights, after the children had gone to bed, she and Luke would play something from their past, something that made them remember when it was easier to be together, and they would dance, slowly and with all the lights out. One night, when Luke had already moved down to the guest room and was packing boxes to leave, he had heard her playing Otis Redding as he walked down the hallway after giving good night kisses to Anna and Ben. He had stopped there in the doorway, one stocking foot on top of the other, and he had looked at her. She had held up her arms, and he had walked into them. They had danced then, revolving together in the terrible tenderness of letting go.

Now, she chose Gladys Knight. And this time it was not about letting go. This time she turned the volume way up high, let it pulse like a strong heartbeat. She let it beat like her own heart, defiant and still strong.

Ben was waiting on the chaise, still curled

around his pain, around his trying-to-understand. She held out her hand to him, pulled him upright. He landed with a little thud on his stocking feet. And grinned, easily charmed. She swept him into her arms, and danced with his legs dangling around hers. She sang "Ain't No Mountain High Enough" loudly, and she felt her voice vibrate through him.

Ben threw back his head and laughed, everything erupting up out of him, laughing out his grief. She kissed the stem of his lithe neck, felt the downy softness that belonged to the newborn she had brought home from the hospital in a striped elf's cap, and then she saw that Anna was there, by the door. She saw her daughter's lips moving. Anna was saying, "I'm sorry you're sick."

"I can't hear you," Jackie said, faking and still dancing. She set Ben down and twirled him.

"Then turn down the music," Anna screamed fiercely.

Jackie cupped a hand over her ear, shook her head: Can't hear a thing. She waved for Anna to come over. Her daughter walked slowly closer, and finally into her mother's arms. Jackie kissed her on the part of her hair, took a deep breath.

"I said . . ." Anna began.

"I heard you," Jackie told her. "I'm not deaf, you know."

Anna smiled up at her, and she smiled down, and then Anna said, "This is one of Isabel's songs."

"Sugar," Jackie said theatrically, "I was dancing to this song before Isabel was potty trained." She smiled. "She may know the words. But I invented the moves."

The children both looked at her in astonishment.

She handed a hairbrush to Ben, the cordless phone to Anna, and she took up a curling iron. Then she picked up the turntable needle and started the song from the beginning. Arranging the kids next to her, she said, "Now, pay attention. Follow me." She began to sing. She began to swing her dance moves around the room.

They both watched. "C'mon back me up, Pips."

"Pips?" they both cried in astonishment.

She moved her arms, her hips, her legs. She coached them, and they were stiff at first, uncertain. But as the music got to them, worked its way down inside the place that hurt and always was going to hurt, they started to react with it.

Soon, they were all three standing in front of the closet mirrors, singing out their whole hearts into a hairbrush, a cordless telephone, and a curling iron. And forgetting what they couldn't change.

ISABEL

She slept without knowing that Luke sat by their bed, straight in a chair, and watched her. She slept deep in her dreams where no one could make her compromise, where she did not have to imagine what Anna's face had been like, hearing those words from her mother. Or Ben's. She did not have to remember Luke crying in the bathroom while he was brushing his teeth, trying to hide the sound of it behind the running water. Isabel slept deep in her dreams where everything was pure and nothing had been tampered with: Grandma Celie still hung laundry on the line while singing old hymns, and Good Humor rocket pops made a day good, and her mother sat on the porch swing and held her, going back and forth, back and forth. Where she was in her dreams, Mama was still there, and Isabel had never been heartbroken and crying because her mother was never coming back. Isabel had never been six years old and falling asleep with her hand in old Matt's fur for comfort. Instead, her mother was still there—in her dreams, when she went down deep enough and stayed a while. Her mother was still there.

JACKIE

It was a short meeting. But Jackie had learned long ago that turning points didn't take hours to happen, nor weeks, nor months. Maybe it took that long for them to evolve, but then it always came down to one brief breath. Turning points pivoted on seconds, nothing more.

Even now, in a matter of life or death, a mere second told her everything. Seeing the doctor's face took only that long, a glance. It said everything. She didn't have to wait for the interpretation of the x-rays on the lighted wall, or the doctor's prognosis itself. She knew. The first round of chemo was over, and she knew.

"There's been very little change," Dr. Sweikert said, so softly, so tenderly.

That's what the disease had done, Jackie thought. It had brought tenderness back into her life, considered tenderness. Since the divorce, she had lived largely on the incidental gestures of her children's affection for her. Her mother and sisters lived far away, and she had never been close to them anyway. Her choices had been so different from theirs. And her friendships were mostly Christmas-card friendships, based only and distantly on shared college dorm rooms and old professional alliances.

Luke accused her of being "closed off." But it was merely that she had a terrible sense of privacy. Luke had been inside with her, once, and the children still were. They offered comfort; anyone else stirred in her an urgencey to hide, to protect her time and her peace.

Her illness had changed that somehow, to a degree. Since she had been forced to acknowledge her illness, she had become ever more reacquainted with purposeful kindness. Charlie Drummond in LA had responded to her requests with unbelievable generosity. The children's teachers had spoken with such reassurance and had been great watching over Anna and Ben for any sign of distress. The president of the PTA had even offered to give Jackie the name of the "wig lady" on Fifty-seventh Street who had gotten her best friend gracefully through chemotherapy. And this doctor sitting across from her could not be any more thoughtful. Even Luke had found it in him, that part of him that he had lost: He was tender again. Jackie's eyes burned to think of his tenderness.

It was the thought of Luke and it was this doctor's kindness now, as much as the news, that made the tears glaze her eyes. She tried to keep them from pooling, from spilling. "So, what next?" she asked. It had only been one round of chemotherapy. Surely there was more to be done. The *Times* was running medical breakthrough stories every Tuesday.

Dr. Sweikert shook her head, as if there were no hope. But she spoke hope: She had another option ready. "There's a clinic in Seattle. Hutchinson Cancer Center. We've studied their process. We like their success rate."

Jackie nodded.

"It's good. The best. They combine some compounds that have been getting results in France, with antibody injections. Seems to activate the chemo."

Jackie forced a smile. "So. Hopeful."

Dr. Sweikert nodded. "It's promising this one. We're upbeat."

On the way home, racing the clock to get to Anna's school for the Thanksgiving pageant that she had spent weeks helping to coordinate, Jackie couldn't get that word out of her mind. Upbeat, upbeat, upbeat. It was like the work of her own heart.

ISABEL

When Luke called to say he couldn't make the kids' Thanksgiving pageant, Isabel picked up the video camera and left the studio. Duncan would never know that she had slipped out for part of the evening. She would just run up to Nyack, shoot the kids performing, and then be back at the studio in time to burn the candle at both ends. Luke wouldn't be home until late anyway.

The kids hadn't said anything to her about their mother's being sick. But they had talked a lot today when she had driven them home from school (because Jackie had another appointment with "Random House," which seemed to have become their code word for The Doctor). Anna, especially, had been a chatterbox, going on and on about her boy trouble, and Isabel had ached for her: the necessary distractions.

Jackie was standing in the wings when Isabel arrived at the school auditorium. She was cuing the school kids for their entrances—all the little vegetables and Native Americans and Pilgrims. Anna was an ear of corn. And if Isabel looked up into the rafters over the stage, she could see Ben suspended on wires, the turkey waiting to swoop down into the role of centerpiece.

Isabel edged up next to Jackie and explained about Luke not being able to make it. Jackie didn't look surprised. But she didn't look all that smug about it either. Which was decent of her.

Isabel knew she could just move into the background and shoot the camera. But something in her gravitated toward Jackie. Something in her wanted another chance. Maybe now . . . She stayed by Jackie and whispered, "I have to tell you something. In confidence." She was hoping it would sound conspiratorial.

"You're having Michael Jackson's baby," Jackie said, never taking her eyes off the stage. She was monitoring the action there so she could tap the shoulder of the next pumpkin or squash who needed to make an entrance.

"That," Isabel nodded, playing along with Jackie's humor (or whatever that comment was meant to be). "And . . . Anna is over her head. With Brad 'The Flame' Kovitzky."

Jackie swung her eyes to Isabel's, interested. "Who?"

Isabel pointed to the stage, to a Pilgrim Father. "See the blond kid?"

"The little Nazi?" Jackie said in a scandalized tone. "Anna's got a crush on him?"

"Big-time."

"This is so depressing."

"What?"

Jackie smirked. "I thought my daughter would fall for someone more interesting. Not one of the Von Trapp family singers."

Isabel grinned.

Jackie was really curious. She said, "She hasn't mentioned this to me."

"She was afraid you'd make a big deal out of it. They've been 'going out' for two weeks."

Jackie was surprised by this news.

Isabel explained, "As you may know, 'going out' in the sixth grade doesn't mean anything. They don't actually go to a movie or anywhere. They don't even eat lunch together. It's just a declaration to the world that they're . . ."

"Going out," Jackie said, adding (and not too unkindly), "Yeah, I had kids of my own. Once." She smiled at Isabel.

"Anyway," Isabel went on, "he walks up to her at the lunch yard today. And tells her, publicly, in front of all her friends, that he's breaking up with her."

"The little shit," Jackie hissed. "In *front* of everybody?"

Isabel nodded gravely, vamping it up a little. She couldn't believe this was working. She was actually dishing with Jackie. Jackie was actually letting her dish. Isabel said, "Which is the whole point of this 'going out' thing. So one of them can dump the other one. And they can imitate the whole passionate adult soap opera tragedy, without ever having to actually date."

"She must be devastated," Jackie said.

"She spent an hour in the girls' bathroom crying." Isabel shook her head solemnly. "I mean, you've got cancer, but *this* is serious."

Jackie shook her head, too. Was there anything more serious (or funnier) than a little girl's first broken heart?

A cornucopia approached her, and Jackie touched up the kid's makeup, then sent the kid on-stage.

"So here's the point," Isabel said, "I pick her up from school today. She tells me the whole story. And asks me what to do."

"And you said . . ."

"Beats me." Isabel demonstrated the shrug she used on Anna. "Ask your mom."

Jackie nodded, accepting the responsibility that had been passed into her hands (and which anyway belonged there). She sent another child out into the lights.

"So she's gonna," Isabel concluded. "Tomorrow. Be ready."

Jackie nodded, and then Isabel scrambled to get the camera ready for Ben's big moment. Suddenly, there he was, a fat little turkey in the sky. His legs were whirling, and his wings were flapping. And finally—boom—a pilgrim shot him. He went limp. His legs dangled. His wings waved no more.

The audience cheered his demise.

"My son," Jackie said proudly.

Isabel got that on tape, too, that look on Jackie's face, those words. Ben would want to see that someday, she thought. It might not matter now to him. But it would. Someday it would.

JACKIE

Thanksgiving had always been her favorite holiday. It was a holiday that celebrated things you already possessed (not what you wanted) and celebrated them with food: bright cranberries and turkey stuffed with chestnuts and sweet potatos pureed with maple syrup. What could be better?

She had gotten up early this year, as usual. But this time, she had taken a cup of steaming cider out to the chairs overlooking the river, which was a first for her. In years past, Thanksgiving morning was nothing but lining food up on the counter for its time in the oven, something like coordinating flights into La Guardia: a lot of incoming, not enough space. She had always been ambitious about the meal, about creating traditions. Luke had told her once, in a scalding tone, that she overdid the holidays with the part of herself that was thwarted by not working anymore. At the time she had been insulted and denied it—because that would have meant that she wasn't totally fulfilled by days of diapers and naptime and noses that need to be wiped. Now she could acknowledge that he had probably been right.

But it was going to be just Jackie and the kids this year for the holiday feast. Luke was going to

Isabel's brother's house in Jersey, and one of Jackie's own sisters was hosting a dinner in Pennsylvania, which she didn't feel up to making. She blamed it on the drive.

She and the children were staying home. Jackie liked the idea of polishing the silver and sparkling up the crystal for only the three of them: her family. She liked the idea of three place settings of the wedding china. When she closed her eyes and imagined it—the children and herself eating in front of the great riverside windows with the sun slanting in—this was something for which she was deeply grateful.

The cider was sweet and spiced with cinnamon. The warmth of it felt necessary in the chill of the morning. She was thankful for both, for the frosted air and the warming cider: for contrast. Also she felt gratitude for the mist rising off the river and dissolving in the strengthening sunlight, and for the last few oak leaves clinging up high, and for what the wind said as it passed through the pine tops. If it had to be the last . . .

No, she couldn't think that. Not today.

She was thankful for experimental treatments. She was thankful for the cancer center in Seattle and for French researchers working with antibodies. She was grateful for flights from Newark to Seattle, direct and leaving soon, leaving tomorrow. She was anxious to start.

Her mind could not go beyond starting, although often now, in a way, its impulse was far beyond starting. Her mind's impulse was on Ending. When she had gone to the butcher for the free-range turkey, and he had said, "Here's your usual twelve-pounder, Mrs. Harrison," she had thought, *the last*? The last Thanksgiving turkey, the last garlic-and-cranberry chutney, the last pageant?

Even the night before, when she and Anna had been chopping vegetables together, when they had been talking about Anna's first boyfriend, Jackie had thought, *Will her first boyfriend be the only one I'm here for?*

She had pushed the thought aside of course, but it was there, circling. And it kept putting itself between Jackie and her best effort to see beyond it and all the way into Anna's inaugural broken heart. Jackie tried to tease her daughter out of her gloominess. She had said, "Did you really think you'd meet someone at eleven that you'd spend the rest of your life with?"

Anna had sighed bitterly, and said, "No, but . . ." Frustration had knitted her eyebrows together. "But every time I'm on the lunch yard, and he's with ten of his butt-kissing little weasels."

"Oh, you don't like his friends."

"They all yell, 'There goes the Virgin Queen' or 'the Ice Princess' or some really clever cut like that. Like it hurts my feelings."

Jackie had grinned, suddenly realizing. "So you wouldn't kiss him, huh?"

"Not with my mouth open."

"Good girl," Jackie had said, before it hit her what that implied. "That means you did kiss him with your mouth closed?"

Anna rolled her eyes. Whatever had or hadn't happened, mouth closed or otherwise, it turned out that it had all devolved into nothing but name-calling. Anna favored *fartface* or *pervert* or "something equally lame." And Jackie told her that the names weren't going to get her anywhere. Only ignoring the kid would work.

Anna had listened closely to this suggestion.

Jackie had instructed her, "He's not even there. You don't see him. You don't hear him. You're just too much of a woman to bother with little boys."

Anna thought Jackie had to be joking. But Jackie insisted that all Brad wanted was attention. When Anna stopped giving him any, he'd try harder for a while. And then he'd give up because it would be no fun.

Anna struggled to get her mind around this concept. She asked, "So I just ignore him? Keep my mouth shut?"

Jackie had nodded, loving her daughter's reliance on her even in matters of the heart, relishing this moment, and then Anna had said, "You think Isabel would do that?"

And that took Jackie aback so much that even Anna spotted it, and she tried to make things better by saying, "I mean, it's just that she's younger. Maybe she remembers how to do this."

What could Jackie do but shrug?

Still, Anna had continued thinking about her mother's advice. "This'll work, huh?" she asked.

"Definitely," Jackie had said, and they had stayed up late together, pouring the pumpkin into the pie pastry and smelling the aroma of it fill the kitchen as it baked. They had gotten out the Irish lace tablecloth and found the silver vase.

Later this morning, Jackie thought as the sun burned all the way down to the surface of the slow-moving river, later this morning, she would fill the vase with asters cut from the fence border and mums from the back garden and some of the fern fronds that were rusting in the shady patch in the corner of the house. And if it was the last time she filled her silver vase with fall flowers, well, let it be a sacrament to Last Things. Let it be an act of thankfulness for what she possessed, what she had this moment, this Thanksgiving, and as she allowed herself this thought, she looked up to see both children coming toward her, Anna holding Ben's hand.

They had on their pajamas and their rubber boots for rainy days. She opened the blanket she was wrapped in and took them onto her lap, and the three of them sat there as the sun climbed higher, and they celebrated Thanksgiving: this moment they possessed. This one moment. Now.

What she felt in that moment, there on the lawn, with both her children held close was the same feeling that made her wake Anna late that night. The kids had been exhausted from the big meal and the big cleanup and the long walk along the river at dusk. They had both fallen asleep in front of the fire, and she had guided them upstairs like two sleepwalkers. It was just as well that they had crashed early, she told herself (lonely for them already), because she had to leave first thing in the morning for Seattle, and she still had to pack. But as she was folding clothes into her suitcase, she happened to look outside her bedroom window, and there in the beam of the streetlight, she saw the first snow falling, so gently.

At another time in her life, it would have seemed absurd to call Colleen over so late on a holiday night to sit in the house while Ben slept. It would have seemed absurd to take her daughter out of a warm bed and go out into a snowy night with their nightgowns tucked into their jeans and under their coats. But now it felt like a sacrament of Last Things. Live or die, this would be the last first snowfall of Anna's sixth-grade year, the last first snowfall of her first broken heart. Every moment was a last moment, an only.

She crept into Anna's room. Her daughter was sleeping soundly, her hair fanned out on her pillow, so fine it even gleamed in the glow of the nightlight. Jackie bent over her. "Anna," she whispered. "Wake up, honey."

"Mom? What's wrong," Anna said, rousing herself with effort. "Is it time for you to go to Seattle?"

"No, it's still nighttime, sweetheart," she said, her heart reaching for Anna, who even in her sleep was aware of Seattle and what was coming. Which was why this was not absurd, waking her so late in the night.

Jackie asked her, "How'd you like to go someplace special with me? Right now."

Anna nodded. She was a little uncertain. She was still heavy with sleep. But she put her feet on the floor and stood. Jackie handed her a pair of jeans. "Tuck in your nightgown," she said.

"We're going out in our nightgowns?" Anna asked, even as she noticed that Jackie's nightclothes were under her jeans.

"We'll put on coats. C'mon."

They drove to the stables, turning off the headlights as they came up the long drive. They shut the car doors silently and crept into the great barn that smelled of straw and dung, such warm smells in the cold of the night. The house beyond stood in darkness. If the Winslows woke, Jackie would explain. Somehow.

It was warmer near the horses, and the great beasts sniffed at them and nosed in their direction. She knew this place so well in daylight that it posed no problems for her in darkness. Jackie giggled at Tomboy's confusion. "You don't know what's going on, do you, boy?" she asked him soothingly as she saddled him up.

"What about Rascal?" Anna said as Jackie led the horse from his stall.

"You're going with me," Jackie said.

She helped Anna up, and then swung herself in behind her. There was a brisk wind blowing across the door of the barn, blowing away the snow and bringing in brighter weather. The moon was full. Maybe that explained her madness, doing this, her sparkling impetuosity: lunacy. She spurred the horse out into the stirring wind and up the path that climbed behind the barn into the woods.

Clouds rose from the horses' mouth, from theirs. They rode through the blue shadows of the trees. And when they broke back into the open, the moon cast the snow-covered hills into platinum. It shone all around them and also in her daughter's eyes. Jackie could see this when Anna turned to smile at her, to thank her that way. They rode for a while in silence. It was like worshiping, being out on a night like this. It was like prayer. She hoped Anna understood.

"This place is so beautiful at night," Anna told her.

The beloved landscape was transformed by midnight and snow and being here together like this. Jackie closed her eyes, memorizing it all—the scent of her daughter's hair, the moonlight, the feel of the cold air on her face—breathing it into her cells, into the very fabric of her being. She believed it would heal her, heal something in her. Surely this was a stronger drug than any in the chemotherapy. Surely this feeling could combat any malignancy. She believed in it.

Anna relaxed into her mother, so peacefully, and they rode until they crested a ridge from which they could see the river below, a current of liquid moonlight. Jackie began to cry then—tears for the beauty of her life when she looked out across it as she now looked out across this gleaming landscape. Sometimes lately, she caught glimpses back over the landscape inside her, which was made of everything she had lived and was shaped by all her memories. And it was too beautiful a place to leave. She could not relinquish it. She could not just go away.

She was careful to keep the tears to herself. They were hers, and did not belong among Anna's possessions. Jackie did not want her daughter to remember someday that she had cried on this night when the first snow fell. She wanted Anna to remember the joy. "I'm never going to forget this," she told her daughter.

"Never say never," Anna said, snuggling against Jackie, sounding happy. Sounding joyful.

Kissing her daughter's head, Jackie said, "There's a loophole. You can say 'never, never.' If you mean it enough to say it twice."

"I'll remember," Anna said. "Always, always."

Jackie held her daughter a little tighter, and she breathed her request, "Promise, promise."

ISABEL

It was probably the most expensive set she had ever been involved in as a photographer. It was almost like making an Edith Wharton book into a movie: The brownstones had been spruced up to appear as they had in the last century. There were ladies strolling with parasols and petticoats. There were men in tailcoats and top hats. All to sell expensive sports utility vehicles to people at the far end of the twentieth century.

Duncan was pacing like sixteen cats.

Isabel knew to the minute what time it was. She was aware that it had taken the crew six hours to set up this extravaganza—instead of two—and that she had been shooting for exactly thirty-six minutes. And she was aware that she had to leave. Now. It wasn't that she didn't have plenty to work with in the camera—on film, on disk. She had just what she needed. Nothing more, nothing less. Unfortunately, she did not have what she needed to make it work for Duncan—which was another six hours to worry it from every direction and waste a ton of film.

She had what she needed. And she needed to leave.

Cooper would break everything down. Isabel grabbed her bag and headed for the Land Rover.

Even before Duncan grabbed her arm, she knew he was behind her. And part of her knew what was coming.

"It's one-forty-five," she preempted him. "I told you. There's no one to pick up Anna."

"You haven't finished."

"I've got it. It's in the can. Cooper can . . ."

"This is my star account," Duncan said heatedly. "I need to offer these clients more choices. A variety."

"I've shot it from twenty different angles. They'll have a variety. Trust me."

His face twitched. "Look," he said. "I'll send a PA to pick up the children . . ."

The last thing she was going to do was let some strange production assistant go after Anna and Ben when their mother was off in Seattle undergoing some last-ditch treatment for rampant breast cancer. "Which part of *no* don't you understand?" she asked Duncan. She couldn't help it. He was an imperious insensitive pain in the ass. She turned and walked away.

He was on her like Lycra. He said, "You're making a career decision here."

She stopped and got in his face. She said evenly, "What are you saying?"

This made him uncomfortable. He softened his tone down to somber. "Isabel, you're the best I've got. Maybe the best I've ever worked with. But these past few months, your work's been slipping." He was having trouble meeting her eye. "It's still good," he said. "But you're losing your edge. Your focus. Your dedication. And your attitude is extremely disappointing."

Isabel felt a pulse of fear in her stomach. She hadn't felt anything like it in years. She was so used to being Fortress Isabel, defended by work, by prowess. "So what, Duncan? If I walk away, are you gonna let me go? You gonna fire me?" She sounded more challenging than she felt.

He looked at her, then away. He nodded slowly, resigned to his decision (even though he also looked as though it might make him throw up). "I'm sorry," he said.

And she believed him. Because he looked so sorry. He looked as sorry as she felt. She bit her lip to keep it from rebelling on her. She looked at Cooper. He nodded. He understood. He was giving her permission.

Isabel turned back to Duncan. "Thanks," she said. And she walked away. She walked away from the best thing that had ever happened to her career, the best thing that might ever happen. Anna and Ben were waiting.

She drove to Nyack. And she had beaten back any and all tears by the time she pulled up in front of the school. She was late, of course, and the only two children in sight were Anna and Ben. They were sitting by the flagpole, and Anna was crying.

Isabel dashed from the car and approached them. Anna was stony in her misery, and Ben looked a little worried about her. Isabel nodded at him and said, "Go sit in the car, Benjamin." He sprinted off a little too eagerly, and she called after him, "Don't drive home or anything."

He snickered over his shoulder.

Isabel sat down next to Anna. Up close, she could see how the girl was seething. The red patches on Anna's face seemed to be throbbing. "What happened?" Isabel asked her.

Anna explained how she was supposed to be ignoring Brad Kovitzky. "I did just what Mom said. And it just got worse. Today he called me Frosty the Snow Bitch in front of everyone."

Ouch. "Men can be such scum," Isabel told Anna. "Your precious brother and father excluded." Isabel looked around. "Is that little bastard still here? Because if he is, I'm gonna rip his heart out."

"No," Anna said sorrowfully. "*His* mother's always on time."

Isabel reached over and wiped away Anna's tears. "Look, I have an idea."

"No, thanks. I don't need any advice from a stepmother."

"Hmmmmm," Isabel said, considering this. "Well, I'm not your stepmother yet. But I do look forward to it with great anticipation."

Nothing from Anna.

"Look, if you're going to pretend you're an adult, then you have to be an adult. Which means you've got to step up to the plate right now . . . and deal with this with me." She studied Anna's profile. "You have a choice. What are you gonna do?"

Anna eased up on her crying and turned to Isabel. She nodded. "Okay."

And when Isabel smiled, Anna smiled back.

Since Luke was tied up out of town and wouldn't be back until the morning, Isabel took the kids straight to the Cowgirl Hall of Fame for dinner. After the pizza toppings were negotiated, Ben disappeared with a fistful of quarters, bent on torturing everyone with the jukebox's thornier selections.

"Okay," Isabel said, laying her hands on the table.

Anna watched her intently.

"Let's start with looks. I know he's handsome. But the best-looking people are so vain. There's always something they're insecure about."

Anna can't believe there's anything Brad Kovitzky's insecure about.

"Does he have zits?" Isabel asked. "We can call him Pizza Face."

Nope.

"Help me here," Isabel insisted.

"Uhhh," Anna mused. "He thinks his nose is too big. But it's not."

"Great, what about his ears? Big?"

Anna considered this. "No, but they stand out a little. Like this." She demonstrated.

"Done," Isabel said, seeing the scenario clearly. "He's a dead man." She struck a pose, providing a model of the Attitude that would be required of Anna. "Monday lunch. You walk up to him. With Attitude. You hear me?"

Anna nodded. She was rapt.

Isabel stabbed her finger at an invisible Brad Kovitzky. Pretending she was Anna, she said, "Hey, Ear Boy!" And she flipped out the ears, per Anna. "Listen up, limp dick, because I'm only saying this one time! So your pathetic no-life, ass-kissing little groupies here better take notes."

Anna is swooning with joy now. She can hardly stay in her seat.

Isabel continued doing Anna smashing Brad: "As for your pitiful knowledge of what a woman really wants . . . I am not wasting my time with

some loser who doesn't even know what snowblowing is!"

"Uhh," Anna interrupted. "What is it?"

Isabel realized—suddenly—she couldn't tell
her. No way could she tell something like *that* to
Luke's daughter, so she said, "Oh, it's an incredibly
disgusting and not remotely sexy thing that they de-
scribed in a movie I'd never let you go to. But it's
real. Does he have an older brother?"

"In high school."

"He'll be impressed," Isabel assured her. "Now,
the clincher is, you walk away, then whip
around . . ."

Isabel showed her how. Tough. Too cool.

"You say, 'The guy I see is in the eighth grade.
And he laughs his ass off every time we talk about
you.' "

Anna's face clouded. "But Isabel, I don't know
anybody at Prep School."

Isabel considered this. Then she smiled. "A suitable boy will be in front of your school. On Monday. At three-thirty. With a very expensive bike.
And he will be a stone fox if I have to call an escort
service."

Anna grinned all over herself and all over Isabel.
She shrieked with delight, then high-fived Isabel.
"I've had the worst day," she said. "Till now."

"Me too," Isabel said quietly. And then she
thought, *Duncan be damned.*

JACKIE

Flying home, she couldn't imagine where she would find the strength to get from the airplane to the terminal, from the airport to the house in Nyack. The cancer treatment had been rough, and the weather bad. It had rained the whole time she was on the West Coast. Lying in the hospital bed, she had imagined that her vitality was washing out of her at the same rate as the rivulets of rain were sluicing down the window. Seattle felt cold to her. She missed home, and the children.

When she had called, Ben had been all absorbed in a failed magic trick, and she could hear Isabel persuading Anna to get on the phone (which galled Jackie, having Isabel intercede that way out of pity). Her children were afraid of her now, Jackie realized. Between her and them, there was suddenly a transparent but seemingly impenetrable wall of fear. They were afraid of how much she could hurt them.

Jackie herself was afraid of how much she could hurt them. This trip had made her vulnerable enough to acquaint her—finally—with the black side of Last Things. It was like another stage of her illness, this acquaintance. She could find nothing to celebrate in it. This treatment was her last chance, and if it didn't work, this was her last trip. And someday, too soon, there would be a last sunrise, a last touch, a last cup of tea. There would be a last time with Anna. A last time with Ben. There would be a last breath. It was not so hard to imagine that possibility now. It was terrible to imagine, but it was not so hard. She had become a believer in finitude. Her own most of all.

The children were so young. Certainly they had grown so far from being merely the seeds inside her that she had nourished with hope and folic acid and protein in every meal. Even when they were in her womb, she had followed with her imagination the knitting together of their circulatory systems and their tiny budding hearts. From all the literature on pregnancy, she had known on which week their hands would form and when their hair would be growing, and their fingernails. And once they were born, she had not failed to notice any of the changes: the first smile, the first fever, the first word. They had both said, "Mama," before anything else, and that had seemed such justification for every sacrifice she asked of herself. She knew the knobs of their heels, the exact pink of their tongues. She knew that Ben had two moles on his chest that made him look like he had four nipples. She knew that Anna had a birthmark on her left shoulder in the shape of a mouth. She knew them from the crease of their toes to the parts of their hair.

And would they remember her at all? It wasn't self-pity that made her wonder. Well partly. But it was more the desire that they should remember somebody who had loved them completely, who had loved them with devotion directed not just at their appetites and their hygiene. Her devotion extended to knowing that Anna colored the sky, always, before coloring the grass in any picture she drew. Her devotion extended to knowing that when Ben sat on the floor watching videotapes, he crossed his big toes, right over left. She knew that Ben was scared of mosquitoes, and that Anna had a strange affection for roly-poly bugs. She knew that Anna pooped when she was nervous, and Ben got plugged up. Who else would ever know them so well? Who but their mother ever could?

She looked out the window of the jet—nothing but cloud cover from coast to coast, it seemed—and she felt trapped in this tube of metal, trapped in the sky, trapped in her fate. And yet, paradoxically, she wanted the flight to go on forever, at least as much as she wanted it just to be over. How could she go home like this? How could she let them see her so weakened? What if this was all they remembered of her? What if this End was all they remembered because it was so traumatic for them?

Her body had never felt this diminished before. Of course she had never been a happy traveler. She was a homebody. So she could blame how bad she felt in part on the cross-country flight and the strange surroundings. But there was a weakness in her that she could no longer deny. And certainly she could not ignore it. When the nurse had taken her to Sea-Tac, Jackie had been forced to rely on a wheelchair to get to her gate.

And when the flight finally angled in over New York City and landed, there was a wheelchair waiting for her at Newark Airport. She stayed strapped in her seat, too weak to protest the indignity of waiting for someone to come after her with a chair.

After everyone else was off, a flight attendant helped her get settled. Jackie prayed that the car-service driver would be waiting with an improvised cardboard sign that had her name written on it in black chunky letters. She hoped he would be a kind man with wide shoulders who didn't speak much English. She did not know if she could speak English just now, did not know if she could string words together at all. She suspected she would need the whole ride up the Hudson to compose herself for Anna and Ben, to make a picture of herself that wouldn't hurt them to remember for the rest of their lives—with her or without her.

The flight attendant pushed her up the incline of the gangway, and Jackie felt dizzy. Her mind seemed unloosed inside her head, wandering off to inspect all the ways her body was failing.

And then she saw the children. They were waiting just inside the terminal with Isabel. Jackie grabbed the wheels, stopped the chair. But it was too late: She felt their eyes on her as though being seen so starkly had a sensation. She felt their horror.

"Surprise," Isabel said sheepishly, standing there with one hand on each of the children's shoulders. She looked as miserable as Anna and Ben. She hadn't expected Jackie to be in such bad shape.

Jackie stood. She willed her legs to hold her, and they did. She willed herself to smile. And she ran, not knowing how she got her muscles to work together, her heart to beat fast enough. She just ran to them and gathered them both into her arms, and said flippantly, "It's a miracle. I can walk."

Anna laughed at this, too long and too eagerly. But she laughed. And Ben covered Jackie with kisses. He could not stop kissing the knuckles of her hand.

Isabel drove, and Jackie floated on her children's chatter. Spent as she was, it was perfect, just listening to everything that had happened while she was away. The news was: The snow had melted. They had baked cookies on Saturday with M&Ms in them. On Sunday, they had gone to a performance in the city where the actors threw food at them (Isabel's treat). And they had a surprise for their mother. She could see that they were squirmy with anticipation.

When Isabel parked in the driveway at home, Anna took Jackie's left hand and Ben took her right, urging her along into the house, where the surprise waited. Isabel followed them in with the suitcase, tramping up the stairway behind them, although Jackie wished she would just go. It was such a strain, being around her, even though she could see the effort Isabel was making on her behalf. It just wasn't comfortable.

"Close your eyes," Ben said when they came to Jackie's bedroom door. He and Anna led her through the doorway.

She opened her eyes. And could not believe them. Arranged around the room, in a chaos of poses, were life-size cutout photographs of Anna and Ben. There was Ben in full magician getup performing magic. There was Anna nuzzling her horse's muzzle. Ben upside down from a tree limb. Anna as an ear of corn. And others. Many others. The sight of them caught in her throat. She struggled not to cry. She managed to say, "Okay, these are good."

It was minutes before she regained her equilibrium. It was the exhaustion, she told herself. It was the drugs. It was jet lag. But, she knew, she did know that what had stunned her was a sudden and beautiful sense of all that belonged to her, of all that comprised her life on earth. And it took her some minutes to find herself again in the wash of feelings.

Isabel had done this for her.

By the time Jackie groped back to her balance, Isabel had disappeared downstairs. She was putting on her coat and scarf when Jackie called to her from the top of the stairs. Isabel looked up expectantly. But Jackie could not tell if she expected to be chastised for having ambushed her with the children at the airport, or if she expected to be thanked for even one of her favors these past days. Instead, Jackie asked her a question. "Could you do something for me?"

Isabel only waited, her face open, ready for anything. Good or bad.

"I'm working on a project," Jackie told her. "A Christmas present for Anna and Ben. And I need you to take some photos of me and the kids."

Isabel smiled incredulously. "You're telling me you haven't chronicled every waking second of their lives on film?" she asked.

Jackie nodded. Of course she had. But there was something missing, a hole she wanted to fill, needed to fill: while there was still time. "I'm only in a few of the pictures," she said. "I took most of them."

She saw Isabel understand. Isabel nodded, then smiled. "I do have plenty of free time."

ISABEL

Isabel had never told anyone—not even Luke—but she thought that her becoming a photographer was all about her mother dying so young. When Isabel was growing up, a favorite thing was to sit with the family albums in her lap and look at the old photographs. They were mostly black-and-white, and there were never enough of them. She had them all memorized. She studied how her mother's hair curled in this one and how her leg was bent here. She looked at her mother's teeth. And then she would go look in the mirror and see if her mother was there—in her.

She understood what photographs were. They were something like sap turned to amber, like words carved in gravestones, like books in libraries: They saved what would otherwise be lost altogether.

Looking through her lens, focusing on Jackie, she thought this, and tried not to think it. And seeing Jackie with her children, it was difficult to believe that she could vanish, that she was capable of not being. Jackie seemed the energy that charged her children, and Isabel had never suspected her of being so . . . so human. Jackie stepped in fresh steaming horse poop, and it didn't faze her. She instructed Ben that he had better wipe his nose yesterday or she was going to wipe it herself—all the way to tomorrow. Jackie threw back her head and laughed with her mouth open.

Isabel noticed all these things, from the farside of her Nikon.

Jackie let her notice all these things.

For a week, Isabel tagged Jackie and her kids around from the stables to the swimming pool to the river walk they usually did either before or after supper. Isabel sat at the kitchen table while Jackie helped Anna and Ben make Christmas ornaments out of pink pepper berries and holly leaves. Isabel got to follow the three of them around in the house where Luke had stripped the woodwork and scraped paint off the beveled glass and hauled the four-poster bed up the carved staircase. She got to peek into what his life had been. She got to peek into what Jackie's life had become without him.

Isabel was never unaware of being *allowed* to be there. She was never unaware that her presence depended on Jackie's having asked for it, on Jackie's complicity. She did not exactly feel welcome. She felt hired. (Which at least kept her mind off of being recently fired.)

At the skating rink one day, while Anna was assisting Ben in his virgin round on skates, Isabel stood next to Jackie at the railing. Jackie's eyes never left the children, as if her gaze alone could keep Ben from falling. She spoke, but Isabel wasn't sure the words were really meant for her. The talking seemed more like Jackie remembering out loud. It seemed like it was for Jackie herself. A kind of comfort. Jackie said, "Ben was born in two hours, went right to my breast, and camped there for three days. Always with this mischievous look."

Isabel nodded. But Jackie wasn't looking at her to see it. She was looking at the children—out there on the ice but also far back in her memory when they were tiny and their world was in her arms, at her breast.

Jackie said, "Somehow his blanket always looked like a cape. Even the nurses said that. He loves to hear that story. Over and over. He was born a magician."

"And her?" Isabel watched as Anna skated by, bent toward Ben's body, hovering over him.

Jackie grinned out of one side of her mouth and said, "Took twenty-eight hours. She just wasn't sure about entering this world." She shook her head. "The doctor wanted to go in and get her. But I knew she would come in her own time."

Then for the first time since they had been standing there, Jackie looked over at Isabel. She looked straight in her eyes. "That's who she is," she said. "Don't let anybody rush her."

Isabel nodded. And she wasn't sure she could speak. Because it was then she realized that Jackie wasn't talking to hear her own memories, to be close to them. She was telling them to Isabel. For Anna. For Ben.

Isabel said, "I'll keep that in mind." It was all she could manage to say. But she hoped Jackie could listen to her eyes, to what they were saying. Because they were promising that she would be like sap turned to amber, like words carved in stone, like light captured in photographs. She would remember these things.

JACKIE

She thought she might be getting like Ben—telepathetic—because one look at the doctor and she had known that Seattle hadn't made any difference. Dr. Sweikert had said how sorry she was, and Jackie had joked about a trip to Lourdes, and the doctor had said there *was* something else, one more thing, but . . .

And Jackie had just waved it off. No more. She was not going to waste her last bit of vigor, her precious moments on a but . . . She was going to have Christmas with her children. She was going to give herself that one last gift.

After she left the doctor's office, she had sat in the car and cried. Cars came and went in the stacked parking garage. She heard couples go by talking. Reverse lights burned in her rearview window, or brake lights. But she sat for a long time and let it come rushing out of her: hot sorrow. She was going to die.

Not sometime down in the dark reaches of time, but on some Tuesday or Thursday or Sunday that was already on the kitchen calendar by the refrigerator. As surely as her birthday was represented there, the day of her death was there, too, waiting for her: a black box, a number, and blank white space. One date. Between now and then, there would be days to go riding with the children, and days to sit in the window seat and watch the snow mount up the gatepost, and days to read to them the stories they loved, and then there would be the day to die. Soon.

Jackie would never grow older than she was now. Her skin would not turn to crepe under her eyes, and her hair would not go white, and she would never live in a house alone and wonder what the children were doing in their lives, in their own homes. She would never see what kind of beauty Anna would grow into or how tall Ben would be when his bones stretched all the way out. She would only have what she had always had—her imaginings of what lay ahead. There would be nothing more.

For a long time, she had cried over these thoughts, and when she finally pulled herself together, she headed for solace. She went straight to the children's school. Isabel was set to pick them up. But every minute counted now for Jackie. Not that it hadn't before. But now she was conscious of counting: counting down.

When she pulled up at the school, Isabel was already there, on time (miracles did still happen). She was standing by her car watching Anna, who was wagging her finger right up in the face of the blond Pilgrim Nazi who had broken her heart. Jackie heard Anna say proudly, "The guy I see is in the eighth grade, and he laughs his ass off every time we talk about you."

Jackie had never seen her daughter like this. Never. And she could tell by the looks on the other kids' faces that neither had they. It was outrageous, extroverted behavior. It wasn't the way her studious little daughter acted, not ever. Looking around, Jackie saw only one person who did not look shocked, and that was Isabel. Isabel looked positively tickled. She looked pink.

As Jackie watched, Anna whirled away from Brad Kovitzky and his friends, and she waltzed right over to this unbelievably gorgeous boy, that Jackie seemed to know from somewhere (but where?). Anna embraced the kid, and meanwhile Brad's buddies started razzing him with their elbows and with wild looks.

"Who in the world is he?" Jackie asked out loud.

Startled, Isabel jumped and turned, noticing Jackie for the first time. She looked caught red-handed. "What are you doing here?" she asked.

"Picking up my daughter," Jackie said. She nodded back at Anna and the beautiful boy with the expensive bicycle, the beautiful boy who was now kissing her daughter's cheek good-bye. And it dawned on her what was going on. "He looks familiar. He didn't do a Calvin Klein ad, did he?"

"Ralph Lauren," Isabel admitted sheepishly.

"What?" Jackie couldn't believe this. She couldn't believe she had just caught her daughter in the middle of such a pageant of deceit. And she couldn't believe Isabel had put Anna up to it. Or rather she could believe it (this was a woman who had been known to wear black-leather pants), but she just couldn't believe it. Not now. Not now when she knew there was nothing she could do to change anything, to rescue her daughter, to rescue her son.

Isabel tried to brush it off. "Nothing, nothing," she said.

Jackie couldn't see how it could be nothing. Her eleven-year-old daughter, abetted by her father's live-in lover, was staging a romance with a New York model who usually made his wages posing in expensive underwear. No way could that be nothing.

But before she could impress this upon Isabel, Anna had arrived in their midst. Her daughter pounced on Isabel, spastic with adolescent excitement even as Brad Kovitzky was sulking away, totally humiliated—because the beautiful boy had kissed his ex in front of everybody. "Itworked, itworked, itworked," Anna squealed breathlessly to Isabel. "Could you *believe* the look on Brad's face?" She jumped into Isabel's embrace, and Isabel hugged her back, but Isabel's eyes were snagged on Jackie's glare, which Jackie hoped was conveying to her in no uncertain terms that, "No it didn't. It did not work."

ISABEL

She could have just gone home. She could have just driven to SoHo and looked up to see the lights in the arched windows of the loft and gone up to let Luke fix her dinner and pour her a glass of Pinot Noir. If Jackie wanted to be bent about things, so be it. Isabel had done it for Anna. And Anna was happy. Anna was thrilled.

But Isabel couldn't take that judgment in Jackie's eyes. It wasn't fair. She could not stand the idea that something she had done out of affection had been twisted into something Evil. It was chewing at her. So she went to the house.

Jackie and the kids were hauling out their boxes of Christmas ornaments. And Jackie was so busy fuming that she wouldn't even look at Isabel.

"Look," Isabel said, "I just wanted to explain."

"Guys," Jackie said to the kids. "Time for you to go upstairs and do your homework."

Anna and Ben got the hell out of there, pounded up the stairs. They knew what was coming.

And as soon as they were out of earshot, Jackie fired a look at Isabel and followed up with a volley of words: "Okay, 'limp dick,' I know. But what is snowblowing?"

"It doesn't matter. I didn't explain . . ."

"Because there'll be, oh, twenty or thirty mothers phoning me in the next hour or so. And they'll all want an . . ."

"Give 'em my number."

"Actually," Jackie said, "they'll want Anna's mother."

That stung. But Isabel fought back. She wasn't going to lie down on this one. "Is that what you're worried about? Looking bad at the PTA?"

Jackie let her jaw drop dramatically, and she looked at Isabel with contempt. With genuine contempt. "You're defending what you did?"

"Right to the ground," Isabel insisted.

"You put filth in my child's mouth."

"Aw."

"You had her lie about that . . . that model."

"Worked," Isabel said. "Like a charm."

Jackie was still giving her that I-can't-believe-you look.

Isabel said, "She was beaten and bloodied. And it was going to keep going on and on. Unless . . ."

"So you became the hero. And I became the schmuck."

And it began to dawn on Isabel what this was about. And it wasn't about Anna saying "limp dick."

Jackie said, "You taught my child that I am a loser . . . who didn't care about her pain."

"That's not what I . . ."

"You think I didn't have some dirty words for that little putz? You think I couldn't figure out some low blows?"

Isabel shrugged. "You weren't passing them out."

Jackie stormed around with the boxes of ornaments. For a weak woman, she was working up a storm of anger. She stopped and looked hard at Isabel, and said, "Maybe you believe in doing whatever it takes to win. I believe that in a crisis, you have an opportunity. For some real growth. If you have to make yourself less to win, have you really won?"

"Oh, please."

"It was a lie," Jackie said. "Winning without dignity or grace is not winning. She has to learn who she is, so she won't cave in to peer pressure, so she can steer her own course . . ."

"She wasn't steering her own course. She was steering yours," Isabel pointed out. "Just ignore him."

"Well that's what parenting is about, little girl. They are pleading to know how to do the right thing. And you sure as hell showed her. And another moment will come, when the stakes are really there, and she will look back on this. And remember how good it felt. How easy it was."

"And she'll stand up for herself," Isabel said. "God help me. What have I done?" Cooper would say she was dripping sarcasm, but how could you fight someone like this.

And now Jackie's voice dropped. It seemed menacing. "You've turned her into you," she said.

It was suddenly clear to Isabel, completely clear. "That's what it is. And that's all it is."

"You've got a point there, for a change. Oh, yes you do." She moved closer to Isabel and stabbed her finger in her face. "You didn't get morning sickness for seven months. You didn't breast feed till your nipples fell off. You didn't spend every minute of every day thinking and worrying that your decisions were shaping the people they were going to be." She paused, dropped her voice even lower. "And you are not what I want my children to be."

The adrenaline of Isabel's anger was still there, but it was being crested by something else, something worse. She considered her words before she spoke. "Look," she said finally, "all year long, I've been watching how you do this: the worries, the sacrifices, the signals you give them . . ." She held Jackie's eyes. "I can't live my life channeling the One True Perfect Mom after you're gone. I can't do it. I can't."

Isabel was defeated. She was defeated by overwhelming odds—Jackie was the children's mother—but mostly by her own sense of compassion. She felt sorry for Jackie, sorrier than she felt for being wronged herself. Most of all, Isabel just felt defeated. But nobody had won here. Certainly not Jackie.

JACKIE

They all three got into Anna's bed, one of them on each side of Jackie. They were propped up on pillows and stuffed animals, and she read to them from *The Secret Garden*. It put Ben right to sleep, of course. She could hear him breathing bubbles, in and out, her slobbery little beast.

Anna kept her head on Jackie's shoulder, and Jackie could feel how intensely her daughter was listening. She was so present. This was the fifth time Jackie had read *The Secret Garden* to her daughter. Anna insisted on it once a year, even now that she could easily read it by herself.

When Jackie got to the end of a chapter, she kissed Anna's forehead and thought of Anna's face that afternoon, flushed with the excitement of spiking a boyfriend's pride, with the thrill of the beautiful boy's hired kiss. Jackie asked her, "Aren't you too old for this?"

"For what?"

"Having your mother read to you."

"Never, never." Anna said, and it was then that Jackie knew that her little girl was crying, so silently and alone. The tears began to soak through the flannel of her own nightgown. She squeezed her eyes tight on her own feelings. She couldn't do that to Anna. She couldn't be anything but strong.

She shifted Anna into her arms, held her so close that there was a pulse between them, one pulse. Maybe her own. Maybe Anna's. Maybe both beating together. And if one stopped, wouldn't the other go on? Wouldn't the one carry them both on from this moment? Always, always?

Jackie held her daughter until Anna fell asleep, and then she held her longer, couldn't let go. She had hurt herself by loving them. She knew this. She had hurt Luke. Their marriage had ended not because their love ended but because she swamped it in how she loved her children. Which was obsessively.

There had been one moment—a mistake—that had changed everything. Anna had been four months old, and she had been running a little fever. But the doctor had said not to worry, just watch her. And Jackie had watched her. Jackie had put the baby down on the living room floor on a quilt, and she had talked on the phone to the office—she had still been planning to go back when Anna was six months old—and she had edited a piece of manuscript revision that her assistant had faxed in, and she had written some flap copy at the computer. And every time she passed from one phase to another, she had checked on the baby, and one time, Anna was blue. She had thrown up and had breathed it in.

All Jackie could think was, *What if I hadn't looked that time? It was almost too late already. What if I hadn't looked when I did, that very instant?*

Jackie hadn't been able to sleep for months afterward. She had paced the floor, holding Anna too many hours of every day. And every night, she had got up out of bed to go listen for Anna's breathing, to touch her and feel the warmth of her skin, to turn on the light and check her color. She had sat in the rocking chair and watched her daughter sleep.

Luke had tried to understand. It terrorized him, too, the thought of what might have happened. But Jackie was haunted by the thought. She was chased by it. She canceled the baby-sitter who was to come—the first ever—so Jackie could go out with Luke and his business associates: Luke had made partner. Jackie couldn't bear the thought of leaving her child with anyone who would be less vigilant than she. Even her vigilance might not be enough. Even her own, her mother's watchfulness, might not be enough to save her baby. So how could she relinquish Anna to anyone else?

She couldn't. And she didn't.

Jackie got Luke to agree to the move to Nyack. Maybe he thought she would calm down in calmer surroundings. Maybe he thought she would settle into motherhood, accept its risks as others did. But it just freed her to be all the more obsessive about it. She had one life: Anna and then Ben. And, given the demands of Luke's role as breadwinner, there was less and less room for him in her one life. It was all in Nyack, centered on Anna and Ben.

Jackie had cried on first days of school. She had gone on every field trip and driven, so her children wouldn't be on that dangerous bus. She had practically chewed their food for them so they wouldn't choke.

There had been therapy for a while, when she and Luke were trying to make the marriage hold. And it had helped her. At least it had helped her. But it had been too late to help her and Luke, too late to save their marriage. That had been over.

It was the worst thing about dying, she thought, as she shifted Anna's sleeping body onto her pillows, and as she stood Ben on his feet and walked him, stumbling and never waking, into his own room. The worst thing was leaving Anna and Ben to live without her as their sentinel against harm. Who would anticipate all the ways that they might be hurt and head them off if possible? Who would think three steps ahead, around the curve, over the hill? Who would have as many eyes as she did?

She tucked Ben into his bed and bent to kiss him. At his doorway, she turned. She couldn't leave. She watched as he turned onto his left side, as he brought the sheets up against his nose and rubbed them there: Ben settling in. She would have known without watching. She could have watched from her own bed, beyond closed doors and walls and with her eyes closed, and she would have seen the same thing.

"God, I will do anything," she breathed into the darkness of the room. She wasn't sure if this was praying, wasn't sure to whom she might be speaking. But if a prayer was an urgent wish, then this was a prayer. "I will go through any amount of pain you give me. If you'll just let me know that they're going to be okay."

Nothing stirred, not even her baby boy in his bed.

"Is that asking so damn much?"

LUKE

Luke got up early. He couldn't sleep at all anymore. He dreamed about the children playing hide-and-seek with Jackie and not being able to find her. They screamed inside his head and woke him. Or he dreamed that he had a way to save her, and the judge ruled against him. When he checked his watch to see how much time his ex-wife had left, the watch was on his wrist upside down. He tried to understand its hands anyway and got more confused. They were crazy dreams.

He thought he would go out Christmas shopping, move around a little, get out of his own head space. He kissed Isabel on the temple. He would let her sleep. The poor love was worn-out on worry. She'd had some big blowup with Jackie over Anna, and she couldn't stop second-guessing herself. It was hard for him to imagine how Jackie could be so hard on Isabel when Isabel had been working in the darkroom so much, helping Jackie with some Christmas project. Every day Isabel emerged with photographs he couldn't bear even to see: Jackie with the kids. The connection between Jackie and her children was as visible as a thick rope to him, binding them all together. And he couldn't help thinking . . .

When he walked out the front door, the streets

were hushed even in Manhattan. It was that early, and he thought that would be great for F.A.O. Schwarz. But when he was in the car, he didn't even head in that direction. Instead, he headed home. (Why did he still think of Nyack that way? Just because that was where his children were, and wherever that was, that was home?)

Anyway, he couldn't face the tinkling plastic extravagance of the toy store on the park. What did you buy your children when they were losing their mother? What present had any meaning at all in light of that one fact?

Driving up the Hudson, he recognized that the season had gone and changed on him. In the city, he didn't notice as much. He woke up in the loft and dressed for whatever temperature WNEW was predicting, and at some point it had become necessary for wool and overcoats. At some point, it was always dark when he came out of work. Even in the summer, he sometimes worked into the dark hours. Now it was relentless. But he didn't really *feel* winter in the city, where there was always a brightness and vibrance that overwhelmed any season. He hadn't felt winter at all this year until just now, seeing the bare tree limbs, stark against the battered gray sky. Until he saw how cold the Hudson looked, like hammered metal. Then it hit him that the days had shrunk to almost nothing, and the year was almost gone. Then it hit him that time was slipping away.

The Christmas trees were already propped at Jack Hope's nursery, he noticed, and he swung the Rover around and went back for one. A big one for Jackie's front window, that big beveled window that had been the whole reason she wanted the house, which had been run-down when they looked at it, run-down and sorry. But that window . . . Luke had always liked to buy smaller Christmas trees that you put up on a box once you had it inside; they were not as much hassle. But Jackie had always wanted them floor-to-ceiling, and that's what he bought now.

She opened the door as he wrestled the thing up onto the porch. The kids were at a roller-skating party, he knew, and he had thought she would be with them. As usual. Why was she here?

Her eyes asked the same thing. Why was he here?

In answer, he nodded at the tree. "Couldn't pass it up. Thought you might need one."

"I do," she said.

She went to sit on the couch, and he knew she was smiling and she was talking brightly, but he suddenly realized that the reason she was home and not with the kids was that she was feeling sick. Today was one of her bad days. Maybe they were all bad now. He didn't ask. He couldn't bring himself to ask.

Jackie had always been the strong one. She was the one who had gotten him through college, like a stake planted next to a flimsy plant. She was the one who had helped him grow straight and tall, who had held him up until he could learn how to do it for himself, until he was strong enough. He couldn't bear to look at her and see weakness. He needed the ferocity of her opposition as he had once needed the ferocity of her devotion. Sometimes he thought he required her judgment of him to judge himself more fairly. She had pushed him toward his own happiness. With her misery, she had done that. And he had found his happiness. And so he believed he needed her.

In one way or the other, he did need her. Not least of all because of the children. As much as he had blamed her obsession with Anna and Ben for the demise of their marriage, he had treasured it. He knew what it was worth. He could see how the children flourished under her love. With them, she showed a restraint in her emotions somehow, and it left them room to grow into themselves. Her guidance, her watchfulness did not intrude upon the children's lives as it had intruded upon their marriage. It was like the air to Anna and Ben. It was like the ground under their feet. It was necessary and generally unnoticed.

But Luke had always noticed. Luke had always known that what Jackie gave them, he never could. She shone on them like sunlight, and if he had at one time wished for some of that warmth himself, he had never wanted any less of it for his children. They were beautiful children. They were bright and sensitive and engaged by their world. They had their mother to thank for that. He had their mother to thank for that.

He got the tree stand from the basement and manhandled the monster fir into it. The smell of balsam filled the air, and through the branches, he saw Jackie with her eyes closed, pulling in the scent of it, savoring it. He used to tease her because she thought she had to close her eyes if she really wanted to smell something or listen to it or taste it. She always closed her eyes during lovemaking.

"It's beautiful," she told him, catching him looking at her.

"How's that?" He stood back to see if the tree was straight.

"Little more to the left," she said.

Luke adjusted it, and then they both watched it, as if it would grow lights and sprout ornaments and suddenly begin to sparkle, as if an angel would fly up and light on its peak. Probably all those things were going on in her imagination. She had that gift.

He looked over at her. She was smiling at him.

Something grabbed his throat again, like a hand's grip, and when he spoke, he had to squeeze his voice through the tightness. "What are we gonna do without you?" he asked.

"You're a great father," she said, looking up at him. "I just never gave you the chance to discover it. You'll be fine." She smiled as though he would be, as if she believed he would be and was bestowing that belief on him as a blessing, a lasting blessing.

ISABEL

Driving up, she was braced for the worst. Jackie had phoned her to meet at the tavern in Nyack, and Isabel knew what that meant: They weren't finished discussing the little episode with Anna and the underwear model, as Jackie so quaintly referred to poor Paul, who happened to be a sweet kid who still lived with his immigrant parents in Brooklyn and maintained a 3.9 GPA. He had even refused to be paid for helping her out with Anna.

When Isabel got inside the place, Jackie was waiting. She looked green, and her cheeks were drawn. She was having a drink, and the waiter queried Isabel with a look as she took the seat next to Jackie. "Patron," she told him. "Double. No ice." She needed some comfort. This was sure to be awful.

She turned to Jackie. "What's up?" she asked, trying to be brave and seem cavalier.

Jackie seemed at a loss for words. She looked at Isabel for a long minute, then she said quietly, "Last year, I lost Ben."

"What?" Isabel knew she said it with a touch too much enthusiasm.

Jackie nodded. "In a supermarket."

Isabel felt stunned. Jackie had to be toying with her, playing her for torture purposes. Every time Jackie opened the door just the least bit, it was only so she could slam it harder on Isabel. *Here, come in and take pictures and listen to what they were like as babies. But back off. Slam. Here, help me when I need to go to the doctor, but then, take this—whammo—how dare you mess with my daughter's delicate little psyche?* Isabel only said, "You're lying."

Jackie shook her head. "I lost him. I was panicked."

"No way," Isabel said. "You never lost that kid for one second. You could find him from a coma."

Jackie held Isabel's gaze. "It's the truth."

Isabel groped around for something to bolster her sense of the way things were: the order of their universe. What was Jackie up to here? She said, "Ben never mentioned it."

Jackie smiled weakly. "He only remembers that I found him."

"Why didn't you tell me?"

Jackie met her eye. "Why do you think?"

The waiter came with Isabel's drink. She took a long, slow sip, trying to calm herself down. Only one thing could be happening here, and it was the most unexpected thing of all: Jackie was actually being human *to her.* Jackie was letting her in, and somehow that was worse. She wasn't sure she could bear to be let in, only when it was time for the good-byes. She wasn't sure she could take Jackie's being kind, if that's what this was. Not now.

Isabel's hands began to shake. Well, at least she would tell it her way, too. She would make Jackie see that she wasn't the only one who had been facing a challenge here. Who still was. Isabel said, "You know I never wanted to be a mom. Then sharing it with you was one thing. But carrying it alone, the rest of my life. Always being compared to you."

She fought her emotions. She wanted a way into Jackie's heart, a way to make Jackie understand that she understood what a huge thing it was to be a mother, what a monumental feat of love. She understood because she had lost that. One day there had been that bubble of protection, that eye on her wherever she was: Playing in the backyard tree or down by the creek or in the ballfield, Isabel had known her mother was watching. Even if it seemed impossible, she knew her mother had been watching. She was safe. And then her mother was gone, killed in a crosswalk by a car going too fast, and Isabel's safety was gone with it. She was six years old, and her whole sense of the world was gone. No one could bring it back, not her poor good father, nor Grandma Celie with her sweet Baptist hymns, nor her brothers or her sisters. No one.

And she wanted Jackie to know that she knew what the sum was, of all that love; she knew by subtraction. But addition was beyond her, and she hadn't asked for this, and she had never wanted to take what Jackie cherished. She had never wanted to take what could never belong to her, not really . . .

All she said, though, was, "It's the Jack Kennedy syndrome. You die young. You always look golden. Perfect. They worship you."

"Me?" Jackie said, arching an eyebrow. "The wuss who wouldn't help her own daughter fight back?"

Isabel looked down into her drink. "Maybe I was wrong on that one."

"Well." Jackie paused. "Maybe you weren't."

Isabel laid both her hands on the table between them. She leaned forward, and said, "I just don't want to be looking over my shoulder every day for twenty years knowing someone else would have done it right, done it better. The way I can't."

"What do I have that you don't?" Jackie asked.

Isabel said, "You're Mother Earth incarnate."

"You're hip and fresh," Jackie countered.

"You ride with Anna."

"You'll learn."

Isabel looked at Jackie, shaking her head. She told the children's mother with solemnity. "You know every story, every wound, every memory. Their whole life's happiness has been wrapped up in you. Every moment."

Jackie's eyes gleamed.

And Isabel didn't know if she could go on. She knew intimately what she was speaking about, what she had lost at age six that still loomed over every major moment of her life. "Don't you get it?" she asked Jackie. "Look down the road to her wedding. I'm in the room alone with her, fitting her veil, fluffing her dress, and telling her no woman was ever that beautiful. My fear is . . . she'll be thinking . . . I wish Mom were here."

"And my fear is, she won't," Jackie said and then she took a long swallow of her drink. She set it down firmly and looked at Isabel deeply. "But the truth is, she doesn't have to choose."

Isabel held her eyes.

Jackie went on, "Anna can have us both. Love

us both." She paused to get her voice under control. "And she'll be a better person. Because of me." She smiled. "And because of you."

Isabel felt her eyes grow hot. She felt how cold her fingers were and how the flesh all along her spine and down her arms had raised itself at Jackie's words.

The children's mother lifted her glass in a toast. "I have their past," she told Isabel. "You can have their future."

JACKIE

Sitting in her chaise by the window, Jackie could hear the four of them downstairs, and it was almost as if she were already nothing but a spirit haunting the home she had loved: a surreptitious angel. She could hear Isabel singing carols with the children, and she could tell by the aroma that Luke was down there making a special breakfast in the kitchen they had designed together years ago, their dream-come-true with marble countertops and an island sink and an immense Garland stove. That kitchen had been huge to them, and in fact their whole New York apartment would have squeezed into it.

Listening to them down below, Jackie watched the river flow darkly through the frosted landscape. It was Christmas, and just knowing what day it was transformed the simplest things, always had. Christmas made everything have sharp outlines. It made voices ring like bells. She closed her eyes and smelled Luke's signature artichoke fritatta, and the rich aroma of it turned her stomach yet made her smile. She was content to have him cooking here again, and only wished she had an appetite for eating anything at all. Everything tasted better on Christmas, too.

Waking earlier, she had heard the children running down the stairs. Ben was chanting to make his wish come true: "a white dove, a white dove, a white dove." Later, she knew, Luke would give him one. Luke would bring in an empty cage covered in tapesty, and when he unveiled it they would all exclaim over what a beautiful cage it was. But Ben would point out that there was nothing in it. And so Luke would put the tapestry over it and unveil it again, and this time there would be Ben's white dove sitting in the cage. With her eyes still closed, Jackie could see how it would be. Anna would clap her hands together once, in quick delight, and Isabel would snap a gazillion shots, and Luke would look surprised himself, as though where had it come from, this wondrous dove. Especially, Jackie could see Ben's exact grin.

She had gotten herself together, after that, slapped water on her face, and arranged herself on the chaise. Very princesslike. Isabel and Luke had brought her a beautiful dressing gown, and she thought it reflected some color onto her poor cheeks. This was Christmas. She wanted the children to be happy.

Her own gifts for each of them were next to the chair. She had told Luke that she wanted him to send each of the children up for their Christmas with her, and then later she would come down and join them all around the tree. But her gift—the only thing she really wanted this Christmas—was the time alone with Ben, with Anna, those few moments. That was all she wished from this holiday morning.

Ben clamored to be first with her. She heard him

call dibs, and then crash up the stairs on his hard little stocking feet. His footsteps pulled up outside her door. He paused, suddenly scared. She knew how scared he was, and Anna, too.

Jackie smiled at him when he opened the door, a strong smile. She had strength for him. She did.

He beamed back, relieved to see she still looked the way she had looked yesterday. She still looked like Mom.

"Hi, honey, c'mon." She patted the chaise next to her. "I've got a present for you."

He bounded over and then sat down gently.

She handed him a package wrapped in his favorite paper. When they had wrapped presents together up here last week, spreading ribbons and tape and rolls of paper from corner to corner, she had watched to see what gift wrap each of the children favored. And she had saved back some of that paper for her gifts to them. She did it every year.

Ben tore through the paper, never noticing it. He did that every year, too. He studied the folded fabric that he had uncovered, then held it up so that it unfurled. "A real magician's cape," he breathed. "Awesome."

She had chosen magical-looking material, all glittery, and with Isabel's help, had turned photographs into fabric, and these were strewn all over the cape, embroidered on with gold yarn. Their whole past—hers and Ben's together—was sprinkled on the cape. Ben was awestruck, looking at them. He swung it onto his shoulders and noticed one picture in particular. It was of Jackie holding him as a newborn. He studied it.

"That's you and me," she told him. "Our first photo as a couple."

He looked up at her. "Did you know I was good-looking right away?"

She smiled at him, her baby. She took his face in her hands and looked him deep in his beautiful brown eyes and said, "*This* good-looking was beyond my imagination." And then she kissed him lightly on his lips. *How many more times?* she thought. *How many kisses left to me?*

Ben was looking at her, and she could see in him then who it was he would become, the man he would someday be. He was already becoming that man. Already, his time had come to begin. He asked her, "Are you dying?"

"What do you think?"

"Yes," he said. "And then I won't see you anymore."

"Well," she said, fighting herself for his sake, fighting the tightness in her own throat and the ache in her heart and the burning behind her eyes. "You won't see my body. But . . ."

He waited.

"It's like when a caterpillar goes away and becomes something else . . ."

"A butterfly," he said.

She nodded. "Just think of me as flying somewhere else. Because as a magician, you know the secret."

He shrugged, not sure he did know.

She leaned forward to give it to him, whispering. "Just because you can't see it, doesn't mean it's not there."

He smiled now, and nodded. He was inside the secret, where she was.

Jackie said, "It might seem like I'm gone. But the magician knows better."

"So where are you?"

She had been waiting for this. For a long time, she had been waiting. She took her hand and wrapped it around his fist, and she held both their hands against his heart. "Right here," she told him. "Right here inside the magician."

"Can I talk to you? When you're there?"

"Always, always," Jackie promised him. "And you won't hear a voice. But in here, in your heart, you'll know what I'm saying."

He looked at her, and there was a trembling in his lips that threatened to shake her down to her foundations, to undo all her careful work with him. For him. "No, it isn't enough," she agreed. "Because it isn't everything. And we want everything, don't we?"

He nodded. They wanted everything.

"But," she told him, "we do get to keep the one best thing we have together, the one best thing we've always had. Know what that is?"

He didn't. But he wanted to.

"Our dreams," Jackie told him. "We can see each other there. You can talk to me. We can go for walks. In cold weather. In warm. In the rain."

He put his arms around her solemnly. He held her so tightly, as if he could protect her. As if it was his turn to protect her, and he was accepting the responsibility. "Nobody loves you like I do," he told her.

She swallowed hard. "Nobody ever will," she said, and kissed his hair.

The bedroom door opened. It was Anna, bringing a cup of hot tea. She searched Jackie with her eyes.

Jackie tried to shine. She thanked Anna for the tea, as Ben hopped down from her chair and spun in a circle to show off his cape. "Look what Mom made me," he crowed.

Anna laughed and moved behind the chaise, and then Jackie could feel her daughter's hands in her hair. The last few weeks, Anna had been doing this, braiding Jackie's hair, finding a way to be close, to be touching her without revealing what was behind it: fear of the day when she would no longer be able to reach out and touch her mother's hair or hand, when her mother would no longer be there to reach for Anna, to hold her close.

"I'm gonna go and show Dad and Isabel," Ben said, spinning again, then racing for the door, where he stopped. He turned around. "Oh, Mom, will you make sure Dad knows how to double-knot my sneakers? The way you do for school in the morning?"

The question shocked her, the practicality of it. He would go on, and she would be replaced. Somebody would take over her functions, what functions could be taken over. He understood this. Hard as it was, he understood.

She nodded. She would do that for him. She would do anything.

He swept out of the room, and Anna came and sat next to her. Jackie picked up the remaining gift and handed it to her daughter. "Merry Christmas, baby," she said.

Anna smiled and opened the present, so gingerly, not wanting to tear the pretty paper. She noticed the paper. She did every year. And when the gift was laid open, like a flower in bloom, she ran her hands over the comforter she found. She ran her fingertips over the photographs stitched onto it, a picture quilt.

"A comforter," Jackie told her. "To wrap yourself in whenever you get cold. You'll have our memories to keep you warm."

Anna couldn't look at her mother. She was safer looking only at the pictures of the two of them together—from her own birth to an outing last month on the horses. She stopped on one special photograph, in which she was three years old and sitting in the bathtub. She smiled, and suddenly her face was filled not only with sadness but with warmth, with light. Already, the comforter was working, Jackie thought.

Anna said, "Remember when it was just us for almost five years?"

Jackie nodded. "It was such a special time. We were inseparable. You were my best friend."

There was something Anna wanted to say. Jackie could see it. But she was having trouble. Finally, Anna looked up at her. "Are you afraid?"

"Not for me," Jackie said. And this was true. She had made her peace with her last moment. "I was afraid for you. But I'm not anymore. Because I know you're going to be okay."

"I don't want to say good-bye," Anna said carefully. "I'll miss you so much." Her eyes filled with tears, and Jackie's own tears blurred the image of her daughter that way, looking at her with such sorrow, the sorrow of truly loving someone.

Jackie drew her daughter close, and they cried together in the chaise by the window. "It's okay, honey," Jackie said. "It's okay to miss me." She pulled away where she could see Anna again. She brushed the tears from her cheeks. "You can miss me. And you can take me with you. When you're in trouble, have me there. When you fall in love, have me there. You can."

Anna's eyes didn't waver off hers.

"That's how we go on, you know. Forever. Because someone takes us along."

Anna swallowed the hardest of her pain. She was trying to be brave.

Jackie fought back the tears and told her, "On your graduation. On your wedding day. When your babies are born. I want to be there. Will you take me?"

"Always, always, always." Anna's voice was filled with the solemnity of vow-taking. This was a promise. It would not be broken. Ever.

They smiled at each other.

Jackie touched her daughter's cheek. "You made my life wonderful."

Anna watched her.

"Take that with you, too," Jackie told her.

And as Anna came back into her mother's arms, back into that deep place of their embrace, and as the silence came around them, the silence of Christmas and of last moments, Jackie felt the single pulse they shared, that one heartbeat that she couldn't distinguish as hers, nor as her daughter's. It was theirs. And it would go on. Even without her.

*T*here is a photograph from that Christmas, a family portrait. Anna would keep it on her nightstand growing up and when she moved into the dorm at college and when she moved into her first apartment and then her first house.

Ben would keep it in his sock drawer and look at it every morning.

In the portrait, Luke and Jackie are sitting with their children on the couch, and everyone is smiling in spite of the truth of that moment, which is that it will be one of the very last.

Isabel is in the picture too, sitting on the end, next to Jackie. She is there because Jackie had said, "Let's get one with the whole family now," and she had motioned to Isabel that this meant her. So Isabel had set the automatic shutter-release, and Jackie had made room for her on the couch.

In that photograph, Jackie has put her arm around Isabel. Her hand is resting on Isabel's shoulder. Isabel is reaching up to hold that hand. By looking, you can tell Isabel is trying not to cry.

Most often, that would be how Anna and Ben thought of their mother. And Isabel.

Together that way.

For Anna and Ben's sake.

With Anna and Ben wherever they went.

Always, always.

AVAILABLE FROM
TIME WARNER AUDIOBOOKS

STEPMOM
2 cassettes/8 hours
ISBN: 157042-6864
$17.98 U.S. /$22.98 Canada